19 March, 1817
Almack's Assembly Rooms
London, England

*T*haddeus Middleton, plain old "mister" in an endless line of plain old misters, considered himself the luckiest of men.

"The first set?" gushed a wide-eyed debutante, gripping her blank dance card in trembling fingers. "Truly?"

"I cannot conceive of a greater start to the evening," Thad assured her and signed his name with a flourish.

She clutched the card to her bosom and all but ran off squealing.

He grinned to himself. Now that she had one name, more would surely follow. Perhaps both of them would find the match of a lifetime tonight.

The first hour inside Almack's Assembly Rooms was always one of the best. He could greet all his old friends, make a dozen new ones, and set the tone for the evening. Like everyone else, Thad was looking for more than a dance partner. He wanted a wife. As for why he was so lucky?

When it came to love, Thad possessed one thing the snobs and the lordlings and the new money hopefuls did not:

Choice.

"Middleton!" A light-pocketed dandy clapped a hand to Thad's shoulder and lowered his voice. "You're not after the Wakefield heiress, are you?"

"For nothing more than a country dance," Thad assured him. "She's yours if she wants you."

The dandy adjusted his cravat. "Then I'll see if there's still room on her card."

Thad returned his gaze to the bustling ballroom before him. Large mirrors between the gilded pilasters along the walls reflected the high energy and sweeping elegance of the *crème de la crème* of high society. A man could not ask for better odds than this.

Technically, he did not yet have a list of potential brides from whence to choose. Or even a single name lightly penciled in on a sheet labeled "…Perhaps?"

But all of that was about to change. *Soon.* He just had to keep looking.

As far as Thad could tell, the moral of most

fairy-tales was to be in the right place at the right time, and not to overlook anyone. One never knew when one's right time and right place would be, so Thad endeavored to be everywhere.

Tonight, he was in the perfect spot for running into Princess Charming. For twelve consecutive weeks during the height of the London season, these hallowed walls housed what was colloquially known as the Marriage Mart. Eligible ladies and gentlemen flocked here every Wednesday in search of The One.

"Do say you'll complete our quadrille," one of his favorite bluestockings said as she swept past. "One tires of discussing the weather with every dance partner, and you always have an interesting book you've just finished."

"This time as well," Thad said solemnly as he signed his name upon her card. "It's about the history of English weather."

Laughing, she smacked him with her fan. "Find another book and meet me for the third set."

"But... the *rain*," he called after her with faux innocence. "We could discuss it for hours!"

Not that he had hours. He was on a mission. If Almack's was the Marriage Mart, Thad had a very specific shopping list: True love. What else mattered?

Surely he'd recognize love when he saw it. Love was impossible to miss. Love felt like the singing of angels and the thunder of fireworks. It was intimate confessions and breathless kisses and riding white horses into the sunset. Love meant waking every morning next to someone as delighted to see him as he was to see her. A fairy-tale come to life.

Or it would be. But first, he needed to find The One.

"Middleton!" Another friendly hand clapped Thad's shoulder. "First Colehaven, then Eastleigh... Must be our turn to shine at last, eh?"

"So I pray," Thad agreed fervently.

Colehaven and Eastleigh weren't just co-owners of the popular and semi-reputable Wicked Duke tavern. They were actual dukes. Moneyed, handsome, eligible ones. Every marriageable young lady in London swooned in their paths.

At least, they had done so until this season, when they'd both tied the parson's knot. Love matches, proving it could be done! For handsome dukes, anyway. Now that they were off the market, Thad's chances had risen overnight.

He glanced about the ballroom at the other men on the hunt. There were elderly but titled roués, feather-witted but deep-pocketed youths, well-mannered fortune-hunters, second and third sons...

And Thad.

No title, but Thad considered not being chained to the House of Lords an advantage. He wasn't astonishingly wealthy, but his annuity would keep a family comfortable for generations to come. Besides, he didn't want to marry some chit so desperate to increase her standing that she'd marry a sack of potatoes if it meant access to a title or fortune.

Label him a romantic if one must, but Thad refused to settle for anything less than happy ever after.

"See my future countess anywhere?" sighed a familiar voice from behind Thad's shoulder.

He turned to give a crooked smile to a friend whose earldom could barely afford to maintain its unentailed properties—which happened to adjoin those of a young lady whose dowry would increase the earl's land *and* his coffers. A neat solution, if only the parties in question had any interest in each other.

"Good luck," Thad said with feeling. Sometimes luck was all one had.

The earl was far from unusual. In most cases, qualifications for "the one" were determined by societal connections, advantageous political alliances, acquisition of wealth, control of property, and countless other practical concerns. And, in most cases, Almack's assembly rooms were the perfect place to solve those problems.

All the familiar faces sailing past came from good families; ladies of good breeding, respectable gentlemen. One needn't fear distressing surprises in that regard, because the patronesses seated upon the dais at the upper end of the ballroom had personally approved every single person in possession of an admittance voucher.

The Marriage Mart was a convenient method of displaying both one's availability and eligibility to interested parties. Indeed, Almack's had been a London institution since 1765. Thad's parents had met within these very walls.

"Card room in half an hour," another friend said to Thad as he passed. "Three card loo. Mortram is hoping to win back the phaeton he lost last night."

Thad inclined his head. He wouldn't be gambling. He wouldn't risk what little he had to offer.

During her come-out year, Thad's mother had been reasonably sought after, and soon had the choice between a penniless baron and plain old mister with two thousand per year. Neither was a love match. She chose the man with deeper pockets.

Thad wouldn't blame any woman for choosing the man with money. Marrying well was virtually the only manner in which a young lady could influence her future. But Thad's mother never forgave her husband for not being a lord, and Thad's father never forgave his beautiful young wife for not staying eighteen and perfect forever.

Neither paid much attention to their son... but Thad had been watching closely.

Theirs was not the sort of match he intended to replicate. Most ton marriages might be political or financial or social, but he didn't need those things. All he'd ever wanted was love.

Despite his parents' unhappy marriage, Thad still believed in romance. And he'd witnessed happy-ever-after... well, secondhand. His cousin Diana had just married for love, following in the footsteps of her parents before her, who had likewise been head-over-heels for each other from the first reading of the banns until the night a fever claimed them, a quarter century later.

That was what Thad longed for. Not just "until death do us part" but "in love from now till death, and forever after." He'd been searching for it for as long as he could remember.

"Did you sample tonight's refreshments?" another friend murmured at his shoulder.

Thad shook his head. "It's always watered-down orgeat and day-old bread."

"*Week*-old by the taste of it," his friend lamented with a sigh. "When will I learn?"

An excellent point. One could not do the same as always and expect different results.

Earlier this year, Thad had realized he'd been placing all his attention on the same pool of ladies. The outgoing ones, the flirtatious ones, the ones who had known him for so long that every one of his dances was promised within moments of stepping foot in a ballroom. Such evenings were fun, but got him no closer to his goal. Worse, he might have spent the past decade skipping over all the most interesting women.

Thad had immediately declared this season the Year of the Wallflower.

By dedicating at least half of each evening to ladies he'd never danced with before, he'd met countless new friends... and no potential brides. But just because there had been no fireworks so far didn't mean he was on the wrong track. In fact, the season had barely begun, and he'd already witnessed two unlikely love matches. Didn't fortune come in threes?

He turned a slow circle, paying close attention to those in the margins. Although gentlemen carried no dance cards, Thad kept careful track. He still had a handful of unclaimed sets. Some young lady here tonight might be the one to spark the fireworks he sought.

There.

An excited tingle of anticipation rushed through him. Dark brown curls, gorgeous brown eyes, dusky pink lips, an enticing combination of soft skin and lush curves wrapped in a gauzy roses-and-cream evening gown.

He knew her name: Miss Priscilla Weatherby. They had been formally presented during her come-out four or five years ago, but hadn't spoken since.

Although a reasonably familiar face at society gatherings, Miss Weatherby rarely stood up for more than a quadrille or two and tended to guard her company. As such, her name had never been linked to gossip—or bandied about much at all. She was almost as much a fixture as the gilded columns and crimson ropes partitioning the ballroom.

Not today. He rolled back his shoulders in determination. After being on the shelf for five years, Miss Weatherby had likely tired of being overlooked by unimaginative lordlings. If she had never danced a waltz, why, Thad would be honored to be the first to ask.

He strode in her direction with confidence and good cheer. Even if no spark marked the occasion, at least they would get a dance out of it, and possibly a few laughs. Miss Weatherby might well become the most memorable set of the entire night.

When he reached the pilaster whose shadow half-concealed her from view, Thad swept a glorious bow. "How do you do this evening, Miss Weatherby? Dare I hope room remains on your card for a dance?"

She gazed back at him with a fathomless expression. "Why?"

He blinked. "Er, because this is a ballroom. For dancing. The food might be wretched, but the orchestra is lovely. Unfortunately, it is impossible to dance a quadrille by oneself, so I wondered—"

"I know what dancing *is*," she interrupted, her dark eyes locked on his with amusement and heat. "Why would you want to do it with *me?*"

Thad moved closer with interest. Now that the conversation had taken such an unprecedented turn, he wasn't certain he wished to waste a thirty-minute set marking out the steps of a quadrille. *Conversing* with Miss Weatherby would be leagues more diverting.

"We needn't dance," he said at once, and gave her a full smile. "I'm happy to promenade, if you prefer."

There was no sense hiding how intrigued he'd just become. Thad did not believe in playing games. Part of being in the right place at the right time meant not ruining the moment by feigning indifference.

She tilted her head. "Did I do something to make you think I'd be interested in perambulating about a ballroom on your elbow?"

"Er," Thad said brightly. "That is…"

"Or did you come here because you judged me to be a wallflower, and therefore desperate for the attention of some impossibly handsome gentleman with courtly manners and a contagious smile?"

Impossibly handsome and courtly manners sounded wildly complimentary.

Thad suspected it was not.

"Er," he said again. "Only a fool would believe all wallflowers—"

"Only a fool," she interrupted, "would assume a woman not dancing must be heartbroken over a lack of suitors. Perhaps the woman received plenty of offers and simply said, 'No.' Just like this."

Miss Weatherby stepped away from the pilaster and into the light, her upturned chin and plump lips suddenly close to his own. "*No.*"

With a flutter of eyelashes, she turned and walked off.

Thad stared after her, thunderstruck. Their encounter had been more sledgehammer than spark, but one thing was certain:

Only a fool would overlook a woman like Miss Weatherby.

CHAPTER 2

here. A satisfied smile threatened to curve Miss Priscilla Weatherby's lips.

Normally she afforded herself five points for rebuffing some wayward pink of the ton, but in Mr. Middleton's case, she hadn't seen it coming —and his devastating smile *was* contagious as sin.

Double points in his case. She doubted many women managed to gaze into those soulful, dark-chocolate eyes and walk away on untrembling limbs. Even Priscilla's normally sturdy knees had gone embarrassingly weak.

Triple points, she decided. That one had taken strength of will.

At least he hadn't taken her heart.

Like most of the gentlemen in this ballroom, Mr. Thaddeus Middleton had a certain reputation.

Unlike many of his peers, Mr. Middleton's reputation was that of a warm, cheerful, fun, kindhearted, sweet, loyal, indefatigably *nice* man.

A peril to avoid at all costs.

She needed to concentrate on the goal. Two more seasons of wallflowerdom, and she'd inherit ten thousand pounds, free and clear. The money was already spoken for.

Taking care to avoid meeting the gazes of unmarried gentlemen, Priscilla made her way around the outskirts of the ballroom to the side farthest from the orchestra. She needed to be present, but not too present. After five uneventful years, she'd thought she had mastered the game.

This particular arena was an easy court to play in. Everyone came to Almack's to see and be seen. Priscilla simply had a different reason than most.

"Who is that?" came a low whisper from somewhere behind her.

"Miss Weatherman?" guessed his friend. "Miss Winterbee?"

"Name doesn't matter," said the first. "Does she have money?"

Priscilla subtly slid to the opposite side of a pilaster. Shadows helped in a situation like this, but not enough. Props were often necessary.

She busied herself not with her empty dance card—to avoid planting ideas in their heads—but with an untouched glass of lemonade. Its presence in her hands made her unlikely to dance, but more importantly, prevented well-meaning gentlemen from offering to refill her glass.

Two points, Priscilla decided when the fortune-hunters walked away without approaching. It had taken no effort at all to avoid them, and besides, the gudgeons hadn't done their homework. She had no riches.

Yet.

She swirled her lukewarm lemonade and gazed across the frenetic ballroom. A minuet had begun, and couples hurried into place. Pale pastels on the debutantes, brighter hues on the married women, the gentlemen all in tailcoats of black superfine.

Personally, she much preferred a round of whist to the call of the dance floor. But entering the card room, even as a spectator, would make her too interesting. Much safer to stay out here, one more swash of pastel pink in a crowd big enough to get lost in. Besides, the card room didn't contain the only winners and losers.

Everyone said the Marriage Mart was a game. To amuse herself on long nights, Priscilla had decided to take that literally.

Everyone walked in the door of Almack's bearing a voucher… and fifty points in Priscilla's secret game. Depending on individual goals, points were won and lost all night long.

Rebuffed at the refreshment table? Minus five. Debutante dancing in the arms of a lord? Plus ten. Rake steals a kiss? Plus twenty for him. Minus twenty for the girl if she was a debutante hoping for a brilliant match. Plus thirty if the lady was a widow in search of fun. Plus fifty for both parties if the woman was an "ape-leader" doomed to a life of spinsterhood.

Priscilla could not *wait* to be an independently wealthy spinster. She would kiss all the rakes she wished, and walk away without a backward glance. Or kiss none at all! Independently wealthy spinsters had far better things to do with their time than provide background decoration in ton ballrooms.

"Excuse me," came a nervous male voice.

Priscilla sneezed into her lemonade and fished for a non-existent handkerchief.

"Just a moment," she bleated as nasally as possible. "It's not catching. Don't worry about your neckcloth. Did you want to see my dance card?"

He did not. He fled as though the fires of Vesuvius were upon them.

Definitely ten points for that one. She was getting much better at fake sneezes.

In order to earn her inheritance, Priscilla needed to avoid all potential suitors whilst remaining unquestionably on the market. She could not lock herself in her chambers for the next eighteen months, and then claim to have been unlucky in love.

The only way to win was to fail spectacularly.

Never let it be said that Priscilla Weatherby hadn't done her part to be in the thick of the Marriage Mart! She attended every Wednesday ball at Almack's without fail.

Since merely being present did not constitute actual participation, Priscilla was no stranger to the dance floor. She accepted dances solely from men who were clearly interested in other ladies, or not interested in them at all—and never more than two or three in a night.

Trial and error had proven this ratio enough to make her Not A Wallflower without being so flashy as to cause her to be an Object of Attention.

During every other night of her uneventful seasons, The Game had been more than enough to occupy her mind whilst awaiting the freedom of her twenty-fifth birthday.

Tonight, however, no matter where she stood or how violently she swirled her lemonade, she could not keep her eyes from Thaddeus Middleton.

He was currently dancing with his cousin, which was sweet enough without even factoring in that he'd taken her in as a ward when Diana had been orphaned five years ago, and under his watch the girl had managed to bring a duke up to scratch.

All the stories about Thaddeus Middleton were like that. If someone was in trouble, he was the first to help. No doddering chaperone left behind, no dance card left empty.

Lest he seem too perfect, Mr. Middleton was also known for his affiliation with the Wicked Duke tavern, a pub teetering on the brink of losing all respectability due to its flagrant admission of persons Not Good Enough for the beau monde.

Plus two hundred points for Middleton and all the other wicked dukes. As soon as she gained her inheritance, Priscilla was going adventuring thousands of miles away from peerage and patronesses. She couldn't wait to be too scandalous to deserve her Almack's voucher.

Which meant Thaddeus Middleton was exactly the sort of gentleman Priscilla would have loved to converse with. If it weren't for unusual circumstances, she would agree to a lot more than a mere stroll about the ballroom on his elbow. Mr. Middleton seemed the sort who would make a marvelous friend.

Her gaze slid to him for the dozenth time since this minuet began. Minus five points for each glance, she scolded herself. And minus fifty for letting thoughts of him fill her mind.

"I saved a spot on my dance card for Lord Raymore," came a nervous voice beside her. "Am I being foolish?"

"Miss Corning," Priscilla exhaled in relief. "Thank heavens."

Finally, something to occupy her besides Thaddeus Middleton's broad shoulders and seductive smile.

Although she did everything in her power to avoid eligible gentlemen, the opposite was true of *in*eligible gentlemen and women of all kinds. Priscilla was sociable by nature, and had become something of a fortune-teller to the debutantes.

All that time spent memorizing Debrett's Peerage in order to know who to avoid had made

Priscilla an expert in who was related to whom and set to inherit what. If a young lady wished to dance with a certain gentleman but had not yet been formally presented, it would take Priscilla no time at all to work out how to make it happen.

"You don't know the marquess," she reminded Miss Corning, "but your brother is friends with the brother of the marquess's cousin, and all four are present tonight. Did you get the dances in the order I told you?"

Miss Corning nodded and held up her card.

Priscilla scanned the names and smiled. "Perfect. When you dance with the marquess's cousin, mention your love of fox hunting. He has a large entailed estate in Norfolk and is passionate about the sport."

Miss Corning stared up at her doubtfully. "I don't know anything about fox hunting."

"Men never expect women to know things," Priscilla assured her, "and you wouldn't be invited along even if you did."

Miss Corning frowned. "Then how does it help?"

"Your dance partner won't be able to hear the words 'fox hunt' without mentioning his cousin, at which point you innocently remark that you've never met the man. He'll be obligated to perform the introduction. Since there can be no greater recommendation than to be presented on the arm of a cousin who has favored you with a dance, the marquess will feel honor-bound to do the same."

Miss Corning wrung her hands. "And then what do I do? How do I bewitch him?"

"No idea," Priscilla replied cheerfully. "I don't know what's *said* during waltzes, I've just observed the steps people take to get there. I've no firsthand experience with flirtation."

Miss Corning's cheeks flushed pink. "I do."

"Then you'll be fine." Priscilla swirled her lemonade. "All I can do is put you in the marquess's arms. The rest is up to you."

Miss Corning marveled at her. "You're the cleverest person I've ever met."

Priscilla wanted to say, *I have to be clever.* A henwitted adventuress won't last a day in the wilds.

But the confidentiality terms of her inheritance prevented her from acknowledging its existence.

"Go on," she said instead. "The minuet is ending. You've a marquess to bewitch."

"Fox hunting," Miss Corning replied and strode into the thick of it.

Priscilla couldn't help but wonder what it would be like to have a romantical adventure rather than devise stratagems for others from the shadows.

Soon, she reminded herself. In eighteen months, she'd be riding across the Serengeti on the back of a sturdy pony and she'd never step foot in a ballroom again. She'd cross paths with a fearless adventurer with the heart of a warrior and the soul of a poet, and together, they'd—

Last until sunrise.

Maybe.

Priscilla's shoulders slumped. If life had taught her anything, it was that all men eventually leave. Even those who loved her.

That was why, from now on, she vowed to always do the leaving first.

Her gaze flicked back to Thaddeus Middleton.

"Minus five points," she muttered under her breath, but didn't look away. "Minus ten, you ninnyhammer."

"What did you say?" came a curious voice from behind her.

Lady Felicity Sutton!

Priscilla could have thrown her arms about her closest friend for distracting her when she most needed it.

"I was talking to myself," she informed her. "Eavesdropping is unladylike behavior."

"All my behavior is unladylike," Felicity assured her. "You'll never believe what I did to my brother's racing curricle."

Priscilla frowned in surprise. "I assumed he was finished racing, now that he's married."

"Bah." Felicity gestured dismissively. "Cole likes winning, not driving. He can always hire someone to race a carriage for him."

Priscilla arched her brows. "I assume it's unbeatable, no matter who holds the reins?"

"A bowl of porridge could drive the carriage,"

Felicity agreed with satisfaction. "It'll be the fastest curricle on Rotten Row."

"I'll never enter a wager with a bowl of porridge," Priscilla said solemnly, then grinned. "What would Colehaven do without you?"

"I guess we'll find out this season," Felicity said grimly.

Priscilla's mouth fell open. "This is it?"

Felicity lifted her chin and gave a sharp nod of determination. "I've had a good run of being a directionless hoyden. It's time to take the Marriage Mart seriously."

Priscilla gazed at her friend in silence.

Felicity was the sister of a duke, and had always been clear about her aspirations. One day, she would marry a rich, titled lord. Someday, she would be a proper matron, commanding a household or three. Someday, she'd become a patroness as respected as any at Almack's.

Priscilla just hadn't expected "someday" to come while she was still around to watch her closest friend walk away.

"I've no doubt you'll find the perfect man," she mumbled. "You're the most splendid woman I know."

It was true. Felicity had already turned down half a dozen hopeful suitors. If she was finally ready to say yes, Priscilla was half-surprised the entire ballroom wasn't throwing rings and roses at Felicity's feet. Priscilla would miss her so much.

"I've no doubt *you'll* find the perfect man," Felicity replied with a grin. "There's no one more splendid than Miss Priscilla Weatherby."

Priscilla snorted. "You do realize you're the only person who thinks so?"

"Then other people are stupid," Felicity replied without hesitation. "You'll find the one who isn't."

Priscilla wished she could tell her she wasn't even playing the game. That she didn't mind at all being three-and-twenty without ever having had a suitor, or even a kiss stolen by a rake with dishonorable intentions. That loneliness didn't bother her because she'd been lonely her entire life. That she refused to *let* it bother her.

Just like she didn't care at all that this set was a waltz, and Thaddeus Middleton was dancing it with someone else. It *could* have been Priscilla's set.

And now it never would be.

"What do you know about Thaddeus Middleton?" she blurted out.

"Middleton?" Felicity lifted a shoulder. "No title, no fortune, no entailed properties. Or property at all. Otherwise, solvent. Good sport. Proper gentleman. Universally admired."

Handsome, Priscilla added in her head, but dared not say aloud.

"Besides that," she murmured instead.

Felicity frowned. "That's it. Some men are exactly what they seem. What makes you think there's something you're missing?"

Priscilla did not reply because her answer

would be, *he's exactly the sort of man I would wish for... if I wished for a man instead of adventure.* Minus one hundred points. She needed to focus on the goal.

"Middleton seems lovely," Felicity said, "but 'lovely' isn't part of my criteria."

Priscilla rolled her eyes. "You'd marry an ancient lecher if he had deep enough pockets."

"Do you see one?" Felicity pretended to scour the ballroom eagerly. "I'll move in tonight. I carry a blank marriage license in my reticule."

Priscilla snorted. She couldn't think of a worse fate than becoming mistress of a household where one lived like a bird in a gilded cage for the rest of one's life.

She intended to travel, just like her father, and his father before him.

Could anyone blame her for being resentful she'd been left behind for being born female?

Papa and Grandfather loved her, though. Priscilla was certain of that, at least. Why else would they have provided for her, in the event she failed to ensnare a husband?

She suspected they *hoped* she would fail at this mission. One couldn't whisk a girl fresh from the schoolroom off to Africa, but a spinster... A spinster could do as she pleased. And what Priscilla pleased was to join her father and grandfather.

"Don't worry," Felicity told her. "It'll be your turn one day."

It *would* be Priscilla's turn one day, but not to stand up at the altar.

She'd been devastated when she'd been left behind. First her grandfather, then her father. A young child, she'd thrown herself into her studies. She'd thought, perhaps when she exited the schoolroom, they would come for her.

They came, but not to fetch her. After her come-out, Papa had told her about the trust established in her name, and the terms of the inheritance. Priscilla understood the message. She needed to grow up first. Once she was old enough to go adventuring, they wouldn't stop her. They'd finally take her with them.

And Priscilla would prove once and for all that women were every bit as capable and fearless and adventurous as men.

CHAPTER 3

"*Please*," Priscilla begged as she climbed atop a stool with her arms outstretched. "I promise I'll be back before supper."

"Promise I'll be back! Promise I'll be back!" squawked Koffi with an indignant flutter of feathers.

He did not come down from his perch atop the tall curtains.

In all their years together, Priscilla had taught her parrot countless words and phrases. *Promise I'll be back!* was the first sentence Koffi had ever spoken. He hadn't learned it from Priscilla.

When her father and grandfather dropped off the golden cage, they repeated *I promise I'll be back* time and again to Priscilla and her new pet to assure the frightened offspring that they wouldn't be alone forever. They *promised* they'd be back.

Priscilla and Koffi were still waiting.

"I'm not Papa," she reminded him now, reaching her hand toward the curtain rod. "I'm just going to the park, like I do every Friday. I always come back for you. But you *have* to wait in your cage."

"Golden cage!" Koffi squawked, inching his little gray feet further down the curtain rod. "Golden cage!"

Priscilla shared his discontent wholeheartedly. She often felt their opulent townhouse with its stuffy little rooms and proliferation of antiquities was nothing more than a golden cage for her, as well.

Unlike Koffi, Priscilla was allowed to fly the coop for short periods.

Grandmother had been very clear: if she caught Koffi outside his cage again, she'd have the maids deliver him to the kitchen to be cooked in the next meal.

"I'll give you a cake," Priscilla cajoled in a singsong voice. "Does Koffi want a cake?"

He glared at her from one black eye for a long moment before resignedly inching back her way. "Tea and cake! Tea and cake!"

Priscilla waited until the last possible second before snatching him from the rod and cradling him to her chest. Koffi was a gorgeous African Grey Parrot, and did not drink tea... or deserve to spend decade after decade behind bars, without ever spreading his wings.

Here in the safety of her private quarters, she allowed him as much freedom as he pleased... as long as Priscilla was home to protect him.

Serving the bird for dinner was no idle

threat. Grandmother had hated the parrot on sight. When Priscilla was ten, she'd been caught with Koffi perched on her finger. Grandmother had ordered him to be cooked for lunch like pigeon.

That had been the one and only time when Priscilla's tears had prevented something bad from happening.

"Now behave," she chided Koffi as she delivered him to his cage.

It pained her to lock him inside. She loved him like a brother. For most of her childhood, he'd been the only company she ever had to play with or talk to.

Before Koffi, there'd been no one at all.

"Tea and cake!" he squawked. "Tea and cake!"

She slid the painted snuffbox from its usual place of honor on the shelf, among her leather-bound travel books and miniature globe collection.

The snuffbox was small enough to fit inside her reticule with ease, and contained bits of pilfered treats from soirées Priscilla attended. Koffi could not accompany her, but she could bring the best parts home to him.

In the wild, African grey parrots ate seeds and nuts, berries and fruit. She took care to select cakes and breads that shared some of these ingredients. Koffi was in England now, but she didn't want him to forget where he was from.

As soon as her inheritance was hers to spend, they would be on the first boat to Africa. They wouldn't have to wait for permission anymore in order to have a real adventure at last.

"Cake for the good lad," she said as she slid a few pieces between the bars.

Koffi nudged all the crumbs into the center of the cage and positioned himself with his tail feathers to Priscilla, as if guarding his treasure from pirates.

Priscilla had never taken back a treat or broken a promise. Mistrust was something Koffi had learned on the voyage from Africa to England.

While he was busy with his cake, Priscilla set about collecting stray feathers from exposed surfaces in her parlor. The maids were aware of Koffi's forbidden freedoms, but the real danger was Grandmother.

Although her grandmother rarely ventured further afield than the primary guest parlor or her private quarters, Priscilla would not risk returning home to a silent bedchamber and empty cage. Koffi was the only member of her family that actually acted like it.

"Unfair," she murmured beneath her breath. "He's here because Papa and Grandfather care about you."

They'd been exploring Africa when they'd heard tragedy had struck. They hadn't made it home in time for her mother's funeral, but they'd brought Priscilla a bird for company and assured her she could join them as soon as she was grown up.

Perhaps a hurried visit during her darkest hours wasn't the fatherly love she'd been craving, but at least it proved they thought of her while they were gone. When she was old enough, they wouldn't have to leave her behind.

Even at nine, she knew her father and grandfather were very busy men. Adventuring wasn't something that could be done inside a London townhouse. The trip to China or India or Africa took months and months by boat, and of course there was no postal service whilst at sea.

And who could blame natural born adventurers for being too busy exploring new frontiers to waste time hunched over a writing desk when they could be astride elephants or camels or wild horses?

Priscilla had read every travel journal she could get her hands on. Even when glimpsed secondhand through ink on a page, the wonders more than dazzled.

By the time her father returned for her, she would be as knowledgeable and eager a traveling partner as any adventurer could hope to have. It would be *impossible* to leave behind a worthy companion.

"Don't worry," she said to Koffi before she quit their chamber. "You're coming with us."

Although one could exit the townhouse without passing through the front guest parlor, Priscilla had never done so. Grandmother spent every daylight hour shuttered in the parlor, and

Priscilla wouldn't dream of leaving for even a moment without saying goodbye.

The front parlor was the largest room in the townhouse. Its tall, wide windows were perennially covered and dark. The Axminster carpet upon the floor had seen little tread. Every surface was as frozen in time as the antiques covering them.

Although the stiff collection of old furniture could seat more than a dozen guests, the only chair that was ever used belonged to Priscilla's grandmother.

As usual, Grandmother's pale hands were folded in her otherwise empty lap. A small fire crackled in the grate, but was unworthy of her attention. Grandmother's ice-blue eyes glared up at the wall at a faded portrait painted the morning after her wedding.

Grandfather liked to jest that the portrait was the longest he'd ever sat in one place.

Priscilla didn't think he was joking.

"I'm going to the park," she said softly. "I'll take two maids with me as chaperones."

She didn't ask if her grandmother wished to join her. They both knew the answer.

Although theoretically Priscilla's sponsor, Grandmother hadn't left the townhouse in years. Priscilla didn't mind. She was used to servants being her only human company.

If their mistress's exacting standards caused a high turnover among the staff, Priscilla would keep weathering that storm, too. New maids meant new people to meet. And besides, once she was an adventurer, she would never remain anyplace long enough to become attached. Hoping to befriend maids and footmen was just silly.

Grandmother's ice-blue gaze slid from the portrait to Priscilla. "Find a husband this time."

This was the only topic Grandmother ever spoke about and, frankly, Priscilla did not understand her position on the matter. Marriage had brought nothing but misery to Grandmother. Marriage had brought nothing but misery to Priscilla's own mother. Why on earth would she want the same thing for herself?

"We'll see what happens," was all Priscilla said aloud.

There would be no husband. Soon, there wouldn't even be Priscilla. She worried every day about how much worse this lifeless, fusty parlor would become when there was no one to interrupt her grandmother's endless, unchanging days.

With nothing but emptiness waiting ahead, why was she so determined to send her granddaughter away, too?

"Find a husband," Grandmother repeated. "Do it while you're still young enough to bring one up to scratch."

"There will be many eligible gentlemen at the park," Priscilla assured her. "Perhaps today is the day I'll fall in love."

"Fools fall in love," Grandmother snapped.

"You don't need roses. You need a husband. Adventuring is not for ladies."

"Adventuring is for adventurers," Priscilla said. "Not long ago, Jeanne Baré was the first woman to circumnavigate the world. And what about Lady Stanhope? A celebrated expert in archaeology. She's visited Israel, Syria, Egypt—"

"Dressed as men," Grandmother said in disgust. "You'll never find a husband that way."

Priscilla did not say *I'm not looking for one.* She and Grandmother were both tired of that old argument. It was easier to just play the game while biding her time for her inheritance.

Grandmother might not be pleased when Priscilla chose adventure over marriage, but she would not be surprised.

"Are you warm enough?" she asked as she crossed the parlor to stoke the fire.

It was a lovely spring day—not that any light dare creep in through the layers of heavy curtains —but no matter how warm it grew outside, the townhouse always carried a chill.

"Find a man with ties to Town," Grandmother said suddenly.

Priscilla poked at the coals with the fire iron. There were any number of reasons for her grandmother's advice. A gentleman with ties to Town was likely to be respectable. A man with ties to Town would not leave it behind.

Too bad it was terrible advice.

Grandfather had plenty of ties to Town, starting with the pretty young heiress who was frozen wide-eyed and happy in the marriage portrait above the mantel.

Papa had ties, too. His mother, his wife, his daughter. Ties were meaningless. Marriage was meaningless. Priscilla had stopped believing in fairy-tales long ago.

The only "happy ever after" was the one you made for yourself.

"I'll be back in a few hours." Priscilla returned the fire iron to its stand, then crossed to kneel at her grandmother's knees. "Whether I marry or become a lady archaeologist, I won't forget or abandon you. I'll write every single week, so you know I'm always thinking of you, no matter where in the world I am."

"Bah," said Grandmother. "Don't write. Find a husband. I know my place and so should you."

"I love you," Priscilla said as she pushed to her feet. "I'll be back soon."

"Bah," Grandmother said again.

This was exactly how this conversation always went, but Priscilla never tired of repeating herself.

Grandmother had never indicated she loved her—*no one* had ever claimed to love Priscilla—but she didn't want her grandmother to ever doubt that at least one person in the world carried her in their heart.

Priscilla rang for her two favorite maids and tried not to be too disappointed to discover one of them had been replaced by a stranger.

It wasn't quite summery enough for the

ERICA RIDLEY

barouche, even with a warming brick, but its collapsible hood allowed one to see and be seen without needing to stop every few feet to allow others to peer inside her carriage.

Being seen was a critical component of complying with the requirements of her inheritance. Priscilla had committed its terms to memory as each delightful word left her father's lips.

If she remained unwed at the age of five-and-twenty, she received a one-time settlement of ten thousand pounds—enough to be independently wealthy.

But to earn it, she must be an active part of the Marriage Mart every season. No joining a convent to kill time. She needed at least three public appearances per week. In the same vein, her name could not be embroiled in scandal. No making herself ineligible by taking a lover or causing embarrassment.

Nor could she speak of the inheritance to anyone, lest she be deemed colluding with a suitor by devising a secret engagement. Nonsensical, since the money would then go to the husband, who could forbid her from walking down the street, much less explore foreign lands.

The easiest way was to remain one of the crowd, familiar but forgettable, always on the outskirts.

Since the ton could be seen perambulating in Hyde Park every afternoon with fair weather, joining the well-heeled caravan was an easy and enjoyable way to put in an appearance without

36

having to dodge waltzes or guard herself from flirtations.

It was also an exceptional vantage point from which to play her game, adding and subtracting points for hearts won and hopes crushed as countless dramas unfolded all about her.

"Miss Weatherby!" A debutante with blond ringlets nearly tumbled from her carriage in her eagerness to whisper to Priscilla. "You were right! He introduced me to the marquess! He's promised to stand up with me at the next ball!"

"Congratulations, Miss Corning."

Priscilla mentally tallied the points: five to herself for a successful plot, twenty to the girl for implementing it, then minus ten for discussing it in plain view of hundreds of people.

Everyone was part of the fashionable stream of carriages, even those who could not procure vouchers to Almack's. The patronesses could keep the nouveau riche and persons with inferior manners from their assembly rooms, but Hyde Park was open to all.

"Miss Weatherby!" squealed another young lady Priscilla had helped earlier in the season, as their carriages drew close. "If you come to my church on Sunday, you'll hear a familiar name in the banns!"

"Congratulations," Priscilla said again.

Five points for her, fifty for the young lady.

Although it was not a path Priscilla would have chosen, she did not believe any person should have the power to dictate someone else's life. Some women aspired to be portrait-perfect figurines trapped in a cravats-and-pearls menagerie.

Priscilla did not begrudge them their schemes and alliances. She thought of her time in London as a prelude to her life as an explorer. She didn't share their goals and culture, just as she would be out of place in Africa or India. There, it would all be part of the adventure.

"Miss Weatherby!" A young lady Priscilla had helped the previous season beamed at her next to her new husband. "I wanted to thank you for—"

Whatever it was she had done, Priscilla did not hear it. There, not forty yards away, sat Thaddeus Middleton atop a smart bay. He looked dashing in biscuit-colored buckskins and a stylish wool coat of olive green. Even his smile was delectable.

"Minus thirty points," she mumbled to herself as the young lady and her husband rode away with Priscilla having no memory of the conversation.

As if he felt the whisper of her breath upon his skin, Mr. Middleton abruptly lifted his head and turned in her direction. His gaze locked with hers, too far away to see the golden flecks in his dark brown eyes, but hot enough to warm her to her toes all the same.

"Blast and damn." She flung herself around to face forward and waved a nervous hand toward her driver. "Go! Go!"

The driver could go, but not far. Hundreds of

other carriages trudged like treacle down the same gravel road as all the others.

She pushed the warming brick toward the maids and fanned her throat. One sighting of Mr. Middleton and spring had turned to summer.

Her high color was due to the wind, not to the handsome rider who absolutely positively was not coming this way, even as her barouche fled inch by painstaking inch behind an armada of horsemen and carriages.

Was she attracted to Mr. Middleton? Of course. She had a pulse, didn't she? But she also had a brain. If she let this foolish attraction go any further, she would lose a lot more than fictional points.

The only choice was to mind her distance and stay far, far away.

"Miss Weatherby," came a meltingly rich, low voice from just outside the carriage. "A pleasure to see you."

The last thing Priscilla wanted to do was look at him again. The mere sight stole the breath from her lungs and filled her pounding heart with dangerous emotions.

"Mr. Middleton," she managed to croak. "Likewise."

There. Was that enough? Would he go away, after having performed his duty by greeting every acquaintance, no matter how fixedly she avoided looking at his face?

"I hoped the fine weather would bring you

out today," he continued. "I was disappointed when I didn't see you yesterday."

Damn and blast. Priscilla's pulse raced wild in her ears. No one had ever *hoped* for her before, let alone voiced disappointment at going a single day without her company. What the devil was she meant to say in response to that?

"I…" Witty banter failed her. "I'm sure you have other people to greet."

"This is my sixth circuit about the park," he replied cheerfully. "If you didn't appear soon, my beleaguered friends would have started greeting me with rotten tomatoes."

Oh, very well. Her high color was definitely due to Mr. Middleton, and not the wind.

"That's a lovely bonnet," he said, his gaze warm and sincere. "The indigo ribbon makes your eyes seem even more luminous than usual."

She would toss the ribbon into the fire the moment she returned home. The bonnet's lack of flowers and ostrich feathers was meant to make her *less* remarkable, not more so. Certainly not… *luminous* to cheerful, happy-go-lucky ton gentlemen.

This situation required a sharp, no-nonsense setdown.

"I like your cravat," she mumbled.

What?

She liked his *cravat?* Brilliant.

Minus a hundred points. Minus one thousand. It was all Priscilla could do not to bury her face in her hands and throw herself from the excruciatingly slow-moving carriage.

If she did, Mr. Middleton would likely catch her in his warm, strong arms and cradle her to his wide, firm chest and—

"Thank you," he said, as if people frequently complimented him on the one item of clothing all men wore, with little variance in location or color. "If you're in the market for a fine neckcloth, I can introduce you to an absolute wizard of the craft over on Bond Street."

He was teasing her, Priscilla realized in wonder. Mr. Middleton was neither rebuffed nor insulted nor bored, but rather having a spot of fun. Not at her expense, but *with* her. As if they were friends.

Now was definitely the time for that setdown.

"Bond Street," she said instead, with a sad shake of her head. "I assemble my own linen by hand, one thread at a time."

"That's because you're a lady," he said solemnly, "and ladies have skills. All the gentlemen I've ever known are helpless as babes."

"Not all men," she assured him. "I believe I read a travel journal once, in which the intrepid explorer wasn't *completely* useless."

"If he *wrote* the journal," Mr. Middleton whispered, "it's probably lies."

Priscilla placed her hands to her chest in faux outrage. "A gentleman? Exaggerating his accomplishments?"

Mr. Middleton nodded earnestly. "It happens

more than you think. In fact…" He sent a furtive glance over each shoulder before leaning close. "I don't even know any linen-drapers on Bond Street. My valet handles that. I was just hoping to see you again."

Damn and *blast*.

Priscilla's voice failed her. Any other woman would have melted right then and there. Come to think of it, she'd actually begun the melting process twenty minutes ago, when she glimpsed him from afar.

Of course she wanted to see him again. Any other woman would be halfway onto his lap by now.

Carnal possibilities aside, he seemed like a man a woman could have a wonderful time with, even when they weren't kissing. The sort that would make a fine lover *and* a cherished friend.

But Priscilla couldn't risk any of that. She'd had her moment of fun, experienced her first flirtation. No matter how rude she had to be to make it happen, it was time to discourage his attentions once and for all. Nothing could jeopardize her inheritance.

Especially not her heart.

CHAPTER 4

$\mathcal{T}$had grinned across the top of his mount at Miss Weatherby.

He hadn't known he was looking for her until he caught sight of her and forgot everything he'd been trying to say to the Countess of Fortescue.

Miss Weatherby was the strangest wallflower he'd ever met. To wit, she seemed only to be a wallflower to *him*, and a handful of other gentlemen of Thad's acquaintance.

He could not help but be fascinated. She was clever and witty, and now that they'd put their disastrous encounter at Almack's behind them, perhaps they could—

"Whatever you're thinking," she said, all the humor gone from her eyes. "No."

He blinked. Clearly the accidental admission that he'd hoped to see her again had been taken in some unflattering light.

"Please do not think me too forward," he said

hurriedly. "I meant to imply nothing more illicit than an offer of friendship."

"I don't think of you at all." She folded her arms beneath her bosom. "And we are not friends."

"Well, no," he stammered. "Not yet. But I thought—"

"Don't think," she said. "I'll save you the trouble. I don't want to be friends, and I don't wish for you to court me. I'm sorry if I misled you."

"You haven't led me anywhere," he assured her, at a loss as to how their lighthearted conversation had turned so sour.

Other than the Marriage Mart, there was literally no reason to go to Almack's. He could probably scrounge up better quality crumbs from between the squabs of his carriage.

Which meant Miss Weatherby wasn't against marriage. She was against *him*. He'd attempted to be Prince Charming and she'd taken him for a villain instead.

This was completely new territory. As far as Thad knew, he had never made such a bad impression before. He wasn't certain where he'd gone wrong, but he *had* to make this right.

"I'm not trying to marry you," he said quickly. "Or seduce you."

Likely an unconvincing argument. Did dissolute rakes ever admit their nefarious plans in advance?

"I know you aren't," Miss Weatherby surprised him by saying. Her expression was kind. "It's not personal. You don't have what I need."

Actually, that sounded very personal.

"What do you need?" He steeled himself for her response. A title? A palace? Money? A knight on a white steed?

"Goodbye, Mr. Middleton," she said instead, and motioned to her driver.

The barouche managed to roll forward three or four inches.

Thad's mouth fell open. It was not quite the cut direct—she had bid him farewell—but it was a baffling end to what had begun as a delightful conversation.

Rather than continue about the park, he nosed his mount away from the flow of carriages and back toward Jermyn Street. His townhouse was not as lavish an affair as the grand residences in Mayfair, but it was home, and he was always happy to be in it.

Lately, however, home had started to feel empty. He handed off his usual trusty bay to the usual loyal footman, walked up the same front steps to be greeted by the same family butler, and then...

Nothing.

Except for the occasional silent-footed maid, the townhouse was still and quiet. Wandering alone down the corridors and up the stairs felt like visiting an after-hours museum of his life.

The townhouse was lonely without Diana around. Thad's cousin had only been his ward for five years, but he'd adored having someone surprising and challenging in the house. They had never been bored.

One day, his home would feel cozy, he promised himself. If not this townhouse, then a cottage in the country. A place and a family to call his own. A wife just as delighted to see him day after day as he would be to see her.

If he ever managed to *meet* the elusive woman.

Not for the first time, he could not help but wonder if his insistence on a love match was merely prolonging the loneliness. Was he a fool to dream of more?

Thad traversed his empty bedchamber and stepped out to the small iron balcony facing the street. The narrow overhang was only one floor up and barely wide enough to fit a footstool, but Thad loved sitting in this nook with a pencil and his journals, or a good book to get lost in.

At the moment, he was in the midst of an enthralling biography on Edward Gibbon. The evening's mad rush from soirée to soirée wouldn't begin for several hours, making this the perfect opportunity to immerse himself in his book.

He settled on his stool with his ankles crossed before him and riffled the pages to find the scrap of paper he'd used to mark his place.

When his cousin Diana had discovered Thad's love of biographies, she had encouraged him to start keeping a journal. Instead of writing about himself, Thad wrote about everyone else. No one but Diana knew his dream of becoming a biographer himself.

A wistful smile teased Thad's lips. He would love to interview someone flashy like Wellington, or perhaps the musicians of Vauxhall, or even Sake Dean Mohamed, who had opened a Hindustani coffee house on George Street before moving back to Brighton. One day, Thad would write stories like theirs.

Until then, he would make do with books written by others.

"Sir? Sir? *Sir?*"

Thad jerked his head up with a start. He was so engrossed in his book, he'd failed to hear his butler until the poor man was practically shouting in his ear.

With reluctance, he marked his place and closed the book. "Yes, Shaw?"

"Her Grace, the Duchess of Colehaven is here, sir."

His cousin Diana!

Thad brightened and leaped to his feet. "Is she downstairs in the parlor?"

"Of course I'm not downstairs in the parlor," came a familiar voice as Diana barged into the room. "I used to live here, remember?"

"You lived in your chambers," he scolded her, pleased to discover that becoming a duchess hadn't changed his unconventional cousin one whit. "This is my private drawing room, to which you have not been invited."

"Mmhmm," she replied in a soothing tone that

implied she'd barge in anywhere she pleased. Diana lifted her arm, from which hung a small basket. "Come along then, and see what I brought you."

New journals, of course. Diana had never presented him with anything else. The timing was quite prescient, as he'd just started a new journal that morning.

Thad hurried after her down the stairs to the main parlor. "Is Colehaven with you?"

She shook her head. "He's at the Wicked Duke, perfecting a new ale."

From the glint in his cousin's eyes, Thad suspected the ale in question was long perfected, and Diana had been the first to try it.

"What's in the basket?" Perhaps it wasn't journals after all, but a bottle of the newest beer.

Rather than answer, Diana settled into a comfortable chair and arched a brow. "How did your hunt go today?"

He rolled his eyes as he leaned back into a settee. "Don't ask. English soil hasn't seen a defeat so embarrassing since the Dutch torched the Royal Navy at Chatham."

"Technically, that was the River Medway," Diana pointed out helpfully. "Yours is still the worst on English soil."

"Lovely," he murmured. "I can't believe I was just lamenting the silence of an empty house."

"Were you?" With obvious delight, she bounded up from her chair and swung the basket onto his lap. "Open it, open it!"

Thad doubted very much that the basket contained new writing journals. He lifted the lid with trepidation.

The low sound of purring greeted him.

Laughing, he lifted a tiny black-and-white kitten from the basket. "Almost exactly what I wanted."

"I surmised as much." Diana's smile was mischievous, but the love in her gaze sincere. "You'll find her, cousin. She's out there. I swear it."

He leaned back on the settee and allowed the kitten to nestle on his chest. It purred with every stroke of his finger.

"What will you name her?" Diana asked.

Thad thought it over.

"Wednesday," he said at last. "At least now there'll be something good about it. One tires of Almack's."

He had never deceived himself on which rung of the social ladder belonged to him. He had enough coin to live well, but not lavishly. Fortune-hunters hurried past, but he was eligible enough and popular enough that perceived interest from him could raise a debutante's credibility in the eyes of other bachelors.

Being used as a stepping stone was perhaps worse than being overlooked. Everyone danced with him, but often only for a boost to reach even higher.

"I'm glad I don't have riches or a title," he said at last. "I want a wife who wants me for *me*."

Diana nodded. Her marriage was a love

match. Her parents had been, too. She understood.

Thad had never seen it; never experienced it for himself. He longed to believe not just that "happy ever after" really did exist, but that it could even happen to him.

But Cupid's arrow had yet to strike.

"Patience," Diana said. "It'll happen when you least expect it."

He stroked the kitten's soft fur. "Who has patience? If love were as simple as fitting Cinderella with the right shoe, I'd drag a cobbler to the doorstep of every woman in town right this minute."

"The only thing I know about love," Diana said, "is that it's never simple. Until it is."

"You are terrible at advice," Thad informed her. "Stop giving it."

Diana lifted a shoulder. "I'm good at kittens, though. We have about twelve more if one isn't enough."

"One's plenty," he said quickly.

What if he did find the woman of his dreams, only for her to turn him down because he was living alone with a house full of cats?

"Don't overthink it," Diana cautioned.

"Says the happily married duchess." But she was right. Diana hadn't found love; it had found her.

Thad had always assumed he would recognize love when he saw it. Now he was starting to worry he wouldn't realize the truth if he stumbled across it.

Perhaps he'd already missed his chance—or even many chances—because he'd been waiting so long for fireworks that he failed to pay attention to little sparks.

"How did you know Colehaven was The One?" he asked.

Diana grinned. "He drove me mad."

Thad snorted. "By that logic, I should be pursuing Priscilla Weatherby."

"Pris..." Diana stared at him. "How can anyone not get on with Priscilla Weatherby?"

"Oh, I don't know." Thad stroked the kitten's spine. "Perhaps it was when she gave me the cut direct at Almack's. Or when I tried to make up today in the park, and she informed me we were not friends and would be nothing more because I had nothing she needed."

Diana's mouth fell open in shock. "Priscilla *Weatherby* gave you, of all people, a setdown?"

"Flaming defeat," Thad reminded her. "I told you."

"But that doesn't sound like her at all!" Diana stammered. "Pris is a dreamer. She lives in her imagination and helps anyone who asks and... Something must be afoot."

"It doesn't matter," he said. "She's not The One."

Diana tilted her head in thought. "What kind of woman *would* be The One?"

"I don't know," Thad said slowly. He didn't

care about looks or money. "She could be anyone."

"How will you know when you find Princess Charming if you don't even know how to recognize her?" Diana asked.

He planted his feet. "What if I miss Princess Charming because I've limited myself to looking for ladies who love jasmine ices and painting still-lifes of flowers, and Princess Charming turns out to be a tightrope walker who skins her own leather?"

She shook her head. "If all you wanted was some chit with a sweet tooth and a watercolor set, you'd have married by now. If you were interested in tightrope walkers, you'd be at Vauxhall every night. You're looking for something different and you need to figure out what it is."

"I'll know it when I see it?" he said hopefully.

Diana's brow furrowed. "How?"

"Easy," Thad said. "There will be rainbows, and bluebirds, and a ray of shimmery, heavenly light, and... er..."

She covered her face with her palm.

"Don't worry," he assured her. "I'll work it out when it's time."

Even the kitten cast him a skeptical look.

CHAPTER 5

*C*links of glasses and cheerful shouts of "Middleton!" greeted Thad as he walked through the door of the Wicked Duke tavern.

He beamed at his friends, passing to exchange words with each one as he made his way to his favorite worn leather chair on the opposite side of the salon. It had won Thad's heart not for its abundant comfort, but for its strategic location. Claiming the furthest chair meant no one would be overlooked.

It also meant arriving at said chair could take an hour or more, depending on what sort of conversations others struck up along the way.

Today when he reached his seat, a crackling fire and a frothy mug of beer awaited him.

"Colehaven's new ale?" he asked as he lifted it to his lips.

Laughter erupted. "How did you know? He announced it not half an hour past!"

"Middleton knows everything," someone else

called out. "He can list the recipes for ale Cole-haven hasn't even invented yet!"

With an unrepentant grin, Thad took a sip of ale and lifted his mug in salute. "The porter he'll reveal ten months from now is even better!"

Good-natured groans filled the tavern, along with another round of clinking glasses.

Thad adored coming here. The familiar mugs, the comforting food, the rumble of voices engaged in a dozen fascinating debates. If there was any complaint to be made about the Wicked Duke, it was that Thad could not bring his journals along to capture each moment in words.

His friends loved him, but they would not understand his passion for telling stories about real people, both ordinary and extraordinary.

Not that it mattered. It wasn't as if Thad imagined himself some sort of author, writing biographies for a living. It was just a funny pastime for those rare moments when he wasn't out in the thick of whatever was going on.

"No promenade today?" one of his friends asked.

"In this weather?" Thad affected a horrified expression. "Have you seen what the rain does to my perfect curls?"

"Perfect mess, more like," said another. "It looks like a ferret has been frolicking in your hair."

"Close," Thad admitted. "The culprit is a kitten named Wednesday. I wanted to bring her, but I feared you ruffians would corrupt her feline innocence."

"Cats are vicious hunters who murder for sport," said a wide-eyed gentleman named Hyatt with a shudder. "Wednesday may be cute and kitten-y right now, but one day you'll wake up with the head of a pigeon on your pillow."

"Spoken from experience," another whispered. "Poor sap still wakes up with nightmares."

"I like pigeon heads," Thad said firmly. "Preferably still on the pigeon. I shall gently advise Wednesday not to store dismembered murder victims inside the townhouse, pillow or otherwise."

"Mmhmm," said another. "Get your gentle opinions in now, because that strategy stops working the moment you take a wife."

"Speaking of which," said a sharp-eyed baronet, "when is the happy day? I've never seen someone spend an entire decade at Almack's without finding *someone* to take home."

"What are you waiting for?" teased another. "Hoping to find a royal princess?"

"Nothing of the sort," Thad assured them. "I'm a simple man with simple tastes. All I require is—"

"Perfection?" said the baronet, with an arch look.

"A perfect *match*," Thad corrected. "Which, fortuitously, does not require perfect people. Nonetheless, I do concede the point. Almack's has failed me grievously on this score."

"What could be more efficient than the Marriage Mart?" asked another. "Have you an alternate plan?"

"Many," Thad assured him. "Extensive research into the art of 'happy ever after' indicates I should either paint my horse white, build a library with a ladder, or seek a vengeful sorceress to enchant me via rose petals and ill-tempered rhymes."

"Start with the horse," another advised. "White paint seems fastest."

"Trot it about Hyde Park a time or two," the baronet agreed. "If no one tosses her handkerchief into the ring, mention your love of ladders, and the impending sorceress. *Something* will spark."

At the mention of a spark, Thad could not help but think again of Miss Weatherby. The spark was there. So was confusion. Things had been going so swimmingly, and then suddenly... not.

If there had *not* been a spark, Miss Weatherby would be much easier to put from his mind. She wasn't just *a* spark. She was a cornucopia of sparks. Dangerous and delightful.

"Look at his face." Nudging each other, Thad's friends exchanged knowing glances. "Almack's hasn't been *completely* useless."

"Or perhaps he knows a good sorceress," whispered another.

"There may have been a spark," Thad conceded. "But I fear I made a poor impression."

"Burned by a spark?" The baronet assumed a haughty expression. "It's not to be stood for."

"Not at all," agreed another. "We're all honorary Wicked Dukes. Are we frightened of little sparks?"

"Hyatt is frightened of kittens," Thad pointed out.

"Be strong," said the baronet. "Try again."

"I've tried twice," Thad admitted.

"Sparks both times?" asked another.

Thad nodded. "Sparks both times."

"Then thrice is the ticket," the baronet said firmly. "This time, pay close attention to all the signs. If the spark is a dud, walk away. But if there's a fire to be stoked…"

"Stoke it," finished the others.

"You lot are very poetic today," Thad pointed out. "Fine use of simile and metaphor. It is only because I wish to encourage such scholarly pursuits that I accept this challenge. If she slaps a glove in my face, I shall return to duel every one of you."

A roar rippled through the salon as its occupants all named their seconds at once.

"Adorable," Thad scolded as he pushed to his feet. "Just for that, I shall duel you all even if the young lady proposes marriage on first sight. From this day forth, a pox on your porters and may all your metaphors be mixed."

Indignant cries and retaliatory curses followed him to the door.

Outside the Wicked Duke, what had begun as

an overcast day had sunk into a dreary, foggy afternoon. Precisely the sort of weather that encouraged lazy fireside debates with one's inebriated friends, rather than quixotic ventures in search of fairy-tales.

Nonetheless, Thad hoisted himself into his gig and directed his horse toward the heart of fashionable Mayfair.

On the way, he passed a flower girl selling daffodils by the bunch. Impulsively, he paused to purchase a half-dozen. They were small, but pretty. The sort of gift that said "Truce?" rather than "parson's trap." He hoped it would do the job.

The edges of his mouth quirked. When Diana had imparted Miss Weatherby's direction last night, Thad had held no intention of using it. Yet his surprise would no doubt be eclipsed by Miss Weatherby's own—as well as that of her fine neighbors.

Despite a one-horse gig being the most ubiquitous carriage in all of England, none would be owned by the residents of Grosvenor Square. Such a conveyance was too common, in every sense of the word.

His bay was respectable, but neither a thoroughbred nor a matched pair. While he *could* afford a flashier ensemble, Thad had purposely chosen not to.

Since he did not yet have a wife to lavish attention and money upon, Thad had been saving half of his income in a special account. One day, he would share everything he owned with his wife. Until then, the accumulating nest egg would allow him to spoil her with something special right from the first.

Unfortunately, this had the effect of making him seem only half as flush as he actually was.

The stratagem repelled more than fortune-hunters, Thad realized as he pulled to a stop before the grand Weatherby residence. Someone used to a certain level of comfort would be understandably loath to lose it.

It didn't matter, he reminded himself. This was what he had and who he was. He would forever regret if he did not at least try to mend broken fences with Miss Weatherby, but if she rebuffed his olive branch, Thad would not be making a fourth attempt to be friends.

A footman rushed from the townhouse to the street, not bothering to hide his obvious shock upon encountering a visitor such as Thad.

"Do you mean to call upon the Weatherbys?" the lad asked in wonder.

Actually, no. Thad had been so focused on *Miss* Weatherby that he'd quite forgotten other Weatherbys would no doubt also be present.

Perhaps the daffodils were a bit much after all. He didn't want to give the wrong sign.

He turned to tuck the yellow flowers beneath his seat when he realized the weather had changed. In the brief moments since his arrival, the fog had mostly lifted, revealing blue skies overhead. Blue skies, and—

"A rainbow," he breathed, staring at the Weatherby townhouse in disbelief.

Rain and sun caused rainbows, any schoolboy knew as much, but it had materialized overhead just as Thad had considered ditching the flowers, and its luminescent ribbon of color seemed to terminate on the Weatherbys' very roof.

What had the baronet said just before Thad left? Pay attention to the signs?

"Sir?" the footman ventured.

"Yes," Thad said firmly, and swept the daffodils to his chest. "I mean to call upon the Weatherbys."

After leaving his horse and gig in the care of the footman, Thad made his way up the precisely manicured walk to the townhouse's front door.

The butler's wonderment at Thad's presence was even greater than the footman's. The poor man seemed at a complete loss for words.

"Mr. Middleton to see Miss Weatherby," Thad prompted helpfully, handing over his card with his free hand. "If the lady is at home."

The dazed butler made no move to enquire.

"I don't care if it's Guy Fawkes at the door," called a wavery voice from within. "Of course Priscilla's receiving."

The butler visibly collected himself and stepped aside to allow entry. "If you'll follow me to the parlor, please."

Thad stepped across the threshold, suddenly less certain he'd correctly interpreted his odd welcome.

For all its grandness, the Weatherby townhouse was dark and full of shadow. Even the air was still and thick, as though the front door had not been used in a hundred years. Thad swallowed.

Perhaps the sorceress had beaten him here.

Each room they passed was a perfectly preserved monument to the opulence of previous centuries. Antiques he had only ever read about filled every room and crowded every shelf.

When he entered the sunless parlor, a small orange fire at one side did little to dispel the sense of unreality, as though he had stumbled into an enchanted castle untouched by light or time.

Indeed, only when his eyes adjusted to the darkness did Thad realize a thin woman with gray-streaked hair and no smile sat engulfed in one of the room's tall Mannerist chairs.

He swept a bow at once. "Forgive me, madam. I had no wish to startle you."

She hadn't moved an inch. Thad's heart was the one beating erratically.

When the older woman made no response, he hurried to add an introduction. "I am Mr. Thaddeus Middleton. I've come to see—"

"No title," she interrupted, "but flowers."

"Er…yes." Thad *knew* he should've left the daffodils in the gig. "That's the short and the long of it."

"Grandmother," came a breathless voice. "A footman said—"

The older woman's hand shot out to grab the edge of a curtain, parting the drapery in two.

A blinding shaft of sun streamed through the opening, bathing a bonnet-less Priscilla Weatherby in heavenly, shimmery light. *A sign.*

Dumbstruck, Thad's arm shoved the flowers in her direction.

"Marry him," her grandmother barked.

"I haven't asked," Thad stammered.

"He hasn't asked," Miss Weatherby agreed, chin held high.

"That is," he added, lifting the flowers, "we could spend more time together and see where things go."

"Which is nowhere near an altar," Miss Weatherby put in firmly, "because we do not have a romance."

"Quite true," Thad agreed. His arm was beginning to tire from holding out the flowers. The flowers were tiring, too. They were beginning to rain petals upon the carpet. "There's no romance."

Mrs. Weatherby narrowed her eyes. "Why are you here, if you're not interested in my granddaughter?"

Thad straightened the daffodils. "Excellent question. Obviously I'm *interested*—"

"—in my parrot," Miss Weatherby said, as if it was not unusual at all for gentlemen to come calling at a young lady's door in order to present daffodils to parrots. "Shall I bring him to the parlor?"

"You *know* I cannot stand the sight of that thing." Startled, Mrs. Weatherby leaped to her feet as if the parrot would arrive at any moment and blind her with its Medusa-like feathers. "Go, go! Fetch it if you must. I'm to lie down at once. You've given me a horrid megrim."

With that, she fled from the parlor with more alacrity than Thad imagined she'd possess.

"I'll send up some chocolate," Miss Weatherby called after her. "I bought the kind you like!"

The only response was the distant sound of a slamming door.

Miss Weatherby let out a relieved sigh. "You made a splendid impression."

"Did I?" he asked doubtfully. "How can you tell?"

"She's left us unchaperoned," Miss Weatherby explained. "There can be no higher praise."

Or a bigger mistake. Thad lowered the flowers to his side in alarm. He wasn't at all certain being alone was a wise idea.

"Maids?" he said hopefully. "Footmen?"

"She probably sacked them all by now," Miss Weatherby said with a pained expression. "She's hoping you'll steal an illicit kiss and feel honor-bound to marry me."

He leaned forward in interest. "You said you weren't interested in marrying me."

"I never denied interest in *kissing*," she mumbled as she turned toward the corridor. She raised her voice. "Come along. This way to the parrot."

"Wait... you *want* me to steal a kiss?" The last of the yellow petals littered the corridor as Thad hurried after her.

She paused at an open doorway and sent him a mortified look that he'd overheard her muttered words.

Thad was very intrigued at the thought of kissing.

"I don't *want* to want to," she hedged, and blushed.

Thad knew exactly what she meant. He kept trying to walk away, but couldn't prevent himself from coming back.

There was nothing he wanted more than to toss his daffodil stumps aside, sink his fingers in her hair, and kiss her senseless.

CHAPTER 6

*P*riscilla's pulse skipped as her eyes met Mr. Middleton's in silent acknowledgment of the electricity between them.

She had dreamed of adventure, yearned for something different, but now that he was standing in her corridor, she had no idea what to do about it.

Something new in this old house! She could scarcely credit it. In the space of a moment, her endless, boring afternoons had been turned on their ears.

Mr. Middleton was the first male guest since... well, *ever*. Other than Papa and Grandfather, of course, who owned the property, despite never being present.

She supposed she could send Mr. Middleton on his way as well, now that Grandmother was out of sight, and maybe she would. But this was also a golden opportunity for Mr. Middleton to discover on his own that he and Priscilla could not be less compatible. She wouldn't have to let him down easily.

He'd run off screaming.

"This is my drawing room," she said and stepped inside.

Mr. Middleton followed her.

Priscilla's heart pounded. She was now up to *two* impossible things before tea time. Maybe ten. She'd lost count.

"Wait here," she said. "I'll fetch Koffi."

She slipped into her bedchamber and closed the door to catch her breath.

"Tea and cake!" Koffi squawked.

"There's no treat," she informed him. "Unless you want to nibble the stalks of what once might have been daffodils."

"Once upon a time!" Koffi squawked.

Priscilla opened his cage and held out her finger.

Koffi stared back at her. "Tea and cake!"

"I'll give you a treat," she promised, "as soon as you meet Mr. Middleton."

"Plain mister, no title!" Koffi squawked. "Plain mister, no—"

"*Shhh.*" Priscilla reached in to pull Koffi from his cage. "Just because a thing is true doesn't mean a man wants to hear you saying so. Be nice to Mist—our guest," she corrected quickly.

On the other hand, this meeting would give Mr. Middleton the perfect excuse to walk away. Papa and Grandfather had no problem leaving Koffi behind. Grandmother couldn't stand the sight of him, or the smell, or the sound. Mr. Middleton would find a reason to flee the second Koffi opened his beak.

With a sigh, Priscilla exited the safety of her bedchamber and returned to the parlor with Koffi perched on her finger.

Here it came. Mr. Middleton would wince at Koffi's screeches, wrinkle his nose to discover grey feathers instead of green, or—

Mr. Middleton was not wrinkling his nose. He was staring at Priscilla and Koffi as if they'd just slid down from heaven on a rainbow lined with gold. Inexplicably, his first words were:

"Better than bluebirds," he murmured, more to himself than as conversation.

Priscilla had no idea how to respond to a comment like that.

"This is an African grey parrot," she said instead. "He's fourteen years old."

Grandmother thought Koffi a filthy creature the color of soot.

"He's beautiful," Mr. Middleton said at once, eyes shining as he bent to Koffi's level. "I'm very pleased to meet you."

Koffi was uncharacteristically silent. Likely because he hadn't heard the phrase "pleased to meet you" since he'd been deposited in Priscilla's arms.

Mr. Middleton held out his finger near Priscilla's.

Turning, Koffi ruffled his feathers and lifted his beak in contempt.

Mr. Middleton burst out laughing. "Was that the avian cut direct?"

"I fear it was," Priscilla said solemnly. "I hope your heart is not broken."

His dark eyes were merry. "At least he didn't say, 'You've nothing I want, Mr. Middleton.'"

Her stomach clenched. She had not wished to wound him.

"Plain mister, no title!" Koffi squawked. "Plain mister, no title!"

Priscilla tensed even more.

Mr. Middleton laughed until tears came to his eyes. "Your sword, it has struck true!"

Slowly, her tight muscles relaxed, and a smile began to play about her own lips. Mr. Middleton wasn't offended. He was *delighted*.

No one had *ever* been delighted over something Priscilla cared about before.

"What's his name?" Mr. Middleton asked.

She took a deep breath. "Koffi."

"Ah." He shook his head sadly. "I'm afraid this is where we must part. I vastly prefer tea to—"

"Tea and cake!" Koffi squawked. "Tea and cake!"

"Exactly," Mr. Middleton said with feeling. "Perhaps Miss Weatherby could go and fetch us some and leave the coffee for herself?"

"Not *coffee*," she said with a laugh. "'Koffi.' It's a Baoulé word. In the village where Koffi is from, sons are often named after the days of the week. I don't know when Koffi was born, but I do know the day he arrived here. I essentially named him 'Saturday.'"

Mr. Middleton looked at her as if he'd been waiting his whole life to hear someone say precisely that.

"At least he's not Wednesday," he said with a strange smile. "One is enough."

"If it *had* been a Wednesday, his name would have been 'Konan,'" she explained.

He leaned back, impressed. "How do you know all this?"

"I actually know very little," she admitted. "But I wanted his first words to be from his own country. I read as much about Baoulé as I can find, which isn't much, unfortunately."

She owed Koffi better than that. For years and years, he'd been her constant companion and best friend, confined to a gilded cage. No one knew her better or had spent more time with her than her parrot. As soon as she inherited, she would take him where *he* was from. They would both discover everything they'd been missing.

"I take it back," Mr. Middleton announced. "I like Koffi better than tea."

"Tea and cake!" Koffi demanded. "Tea and cake!"

"I never said I liked you better than cakes," Mr. Middleton whispered. "A gentleman must know his weaknesses."

Priscilla giggled despite herself. She could not believe that the gentleman in her drawing room was spending as much time in conversation with her parrot as with her—or that it was the exact right thing to do. Having him with them was so much better than her and Koffi sitting around alone.

"Can he fly?" Mr. Middleton asked.

She lifted her hand high overhead. "Goodbye, Koffi."

"Goodbye, my love! ¡Adios, mi amor! *Merde!*" Koffi squawked as he flew to the curtain rod atop the closest window.

"Forgive me, but…" Mr. Middleton's brown eyes danced with humor. "How certain are you as to the accuracy of his translations?"

Priscilla widened her eyes. "Are you insinuating my prized parrot is anything less than fully fluent?"

"'Insinuate?'" he gasped with faux affront. "Dear lady, I swear this truth to you upon my soul. You have been hoodwinked most foully!" He paused and tilted his head. "Fowl-ly?"

She took a step closer. "How can you be so sure?"

"There has never been a surer creature than I," he assured her, coming nearer until their toes nearly touched. "French is the language of love, my dear, and I am an expert in…"

"Love?" she whispered, as the tips of her fingers brushed his.

"I was going to say 'conjugating verbs,'" he whispered, "but my *second*-best marks were always in—"

"Beast." She gave him a light slap on his chest.

He trapped her hand between his own and the beating of his heart. His head lowered toward hers. *"Je veux ce que je n'ose pas avoir."*

She licked her lips. They were too close to his, the temptation too much to bear, but she could not pull away.

"Only my parrot speaks French," she forced herself to say lightly, breaking the spell.

He smiled, slow and heartbreaking, and dropped her hand. "That's how the French say, 'My bear drinks beer in the ballroom.' A very useful phrase."

Priscilla pressed her trembling palm to her too-rapid heart and turned her gaze away. That wasn't what he'd said at all. She'd studied just enough to recognize, *I want what I dare not have.*

If he'd touched her for a single second longer, she probably would have given everything to him. Her pulse still hadn't calmed.

To distract them both from how close she'd come to willingly surrendering a kiss, she quickly sought for an innocent new subject. "Were you out at Hyde Park this afternoon?"

"I was not," he said, relaxing visibly at the much safer topic. "I was far too busy doing very important gentlemanly things to spare a moment for the park."

She narrowed her eyes in suspicion.

"You were at your club?" she guessed.

"Tavern," he corrected. "Clubs are for people with fortunes or titles. Ask your parrot."

"Koffi would never visit a common tavern," she assured him. "Which one is yours?"

"The Wicked Duke, over on Haymarket," he said at once. "It's a barely reputable affair, what with allowing riff-raff like myself, but it *is* owned by Eastleigh—"

"Valentine Fairfax, sixth Duke of Eastleigh." Koffi flapped his wings.

Mr. Middleton blinked. "Er... yes. And also Colehaven—"

"Caleb Sutton, fifth Duke of Colehaven," Koffi squawked.

Mr. Middleton cut an astonished glance toward Priscilla.

Her cheeks heated. "He *may* have listened to the entirety of *Debrett's Peerage* on multiple occasions."

Priscilla often studied out loud. It was the only way to banish her home's endless silence, even for a moment.

"Have you considered a novel?" Mr. Middleton asked politely. "If he's going to repeat everything he hears, at least Koffi could say things like, 'To the University of Oxford, I acknowledge no obligation,' and then your guests can debate amongst themselves whether Koffi is casting aspersions upon that honored institution or jealous over being denied admission."

She folded her arms beneath her breasts. "Is that from a novel?"

"Biography," he admitted. "Edward Gibbon,

compiled by Lord Sheffield. And to answer your next question… no, he was not a parrot."

"Pity," she said sadly. "If he were, I might've read his biography."

"Do you not read them?" Mr. Middleton exclaimed in obvious horror. "You haven't any clue what you're missing. Good biographies are fascinating to read, even when the subject is an ordinary human."

"Spoken like a man who does not have a pet," Priscilla said with a sniff.

"I do, indeed." He drew himself upright. "I have the fiercest, deadliest, six-week-old kitten London has ever seen. I'm told she'll start murdering pigeons any day now. She would make an excellent biography."

"She's six weeks old," Priscilla said with a laugh. "She hasn't had enough life yet to start thinking about biographies. Besides, she and Koffi are doomed never to meet."

Mr. Middleton gaped at her. "What— How can you— Romeo and Juliet never faced a villain so cruel!"

"She's a *cat*," Priscilla reminded him. "Koffi is a bird. Don't you find that more than star-crossed?"

"My cat loves everyone," he protested. "I've only had her for one day, but I'm certain she would treat Koffi with decorum and grace."

"Koffi is unlikely to return the favor," she informed him sadly. "He is an adventurer by blood, just like my father and grandfather."

"Are they adventurers?" he asked with interest. "Those are among my favorite biographies."

"Mine, too," she admitted.

His mouth fell open. "You *have* read good books."

"A couple." She gestured to her bookshelves, which overflowed with tomes and atlases from around the world.

His eyes widened in appreciation. "Your father and grandfather must have marvelous stories."

"They do," she gushed at once, pushing away the tiny little voice reminding her she'd heard very few of them. "My grandfather fell in love with adventure during his Grand Tour when he was young. He said my grandmother's beauty was the one thing capable of luring him from adventure."

Mr. Middleton's eyes brightened. "Is he here now?"

"N-no," she admitted. "But he comes back... sometimes."

Once, when she was nine. And once, when she was seventeen.

"And your father?" Mr. Middleton asked.

Present on those same two occasions, but not for her birth, her come-out, or any day after.

They were busy, Priscilla reminded herself. Africa wasn't around the corner. As soon as she was a free woman, she could join them on their travels, and it would no longer matter how much time they had once spent apart.

"Father is Grandfather's traveling companion," she said. "They brought Koffi from Africa. Their lives are full of nothing but adventure."

She expected Mr. Middleton to say, *It would make a splendid biography.*

"That must be hard on their wives," he said softly instead. "And on you."

To Priscilla's horror, the backs of her eyes pricked with heat and she quickly glanced away.

No one had *ever* acknowledged the impact on Priscilla. She had a home. She had "good blood." She had a parrot. What did she possibly have to complain about? A child cannot understand *real* loss, as Grandmother was fond of saying.

Perhaps that was why she heard herself say, "Grandmother never left the house again."

At first, it was because she wanted to be home to greet her husband, whenever he might return. When that didn't happen, she focused all her attention on her young son, who grew to be the spitting image of his father in every way.

When Papa left to join his father on adventure, leaving a pregnant young wife at home, Grandmother could not leave the house to visit in sympathy—so she welcomed her daughter-in-law into her home instead.

It was as if, even then, Grandmother knew the men would not return.

Mother hadn't known it. She thought she was different. Pretty enough. Doting enough. *Pregnant* enough to cause him to stay, if only for a while.

They didn't even come home for the funeral.

"Mother died of a broken heart," Priscilla said at last. It was close enough to the truth. "When I go adventuring, I will take care not to leave anyone who loves me behind."

That was the dual danger of a husband. Either he would leave her first, off on adventure... or when Priscilla came home from hers, she would find only a carved stone to mark his memory.

Mr. Middleton's warm brown eyes did not waver from hers.

"After all that," he said softly, "You still mean to go adventuring?"

She nodded, the movement jerky. Of course she meant to go. Had been dreaming of the day ever since she was a small child. She couldn't wait to set out. Adventuring must be the very best thing in all the world. What other reason could there be for Papa and Grandfather to leave her behind?

"I made a promise," she said. "I'm taking Koffi to Baoulé to see his native homeland."

Koffi flapped his wings. "Goodbye, my love! ¡Adios, mi amor! *Merde!*"

The misquote didn't make her smile. It never did. It was how she would feel in the moment if her best friend chose to fly away.

"That... sounds like an incredible adventure," Mr. Middleton admitted. "Well worth a biography."

"Not yet," she said with a crooked smile. "So far, I haven't been anywhere but London."

"I didn't mean you," he assured her. "Koffi has a heart-rending tale of being wrenched from his homeland, only to be returned by the one person who loves him most. He's also a gorgeous specimen, and a stunning conversationalist, what with his command of three languages."

She lifted her chin. "Who do you think taught him those languages?"

"Not a girl," he said in horror, *"obviously*. It would hurt their little brains to think of anything other than bonnets and buttons. As I say to all my friends at the Wicked Duke, Oxford would be far better off admitting parrots than to open its doors to the likes of—"

She shoved his chest with a laugh. *"Vaya al diablo, hijo de—"*

"Oh, your words! How they wound!" He clutched his heart, crushing his cravat in the process. *"Je ne suis qu'un pauvre garçon. Ma langue n'est pas aussi sage que mon cœur."*

She narrowed her eyes, then growled in defeat. "Too fast. Say it again?"

He waved a careless hand. "Nothing, nothing. Just some drivel about the fog and... how fog-like the fog can be. Especially in London."

"I mean it." She stepped closer. "I can read French almost as well as English, but I've never heard anyone but myself pronounce it."

"And Koffi," he reminded her. "He can *hear* you."

She lowered her voice conspiratorially. "Koffi's accent is even worse than mine. We're probably tied with grammar."

To her surprise, Mr. Middleton did not laugh. He tilted his head and regarded her seriously. "How much do you know?"

"Vocabulary? Quite a bit of it. I've memorized every list I can get my hands on. Grammar? Just what I can puzzle out from books. I've never had a proper tutor, and poring over Voltaire and Beaumarchais line by line isn't the best way to—"

"I'll write you letters," Mr. Middleton said without hesitation. "Once in the morning, and once before I retire. You'll have context, because you know what we've discussed before. All the same, I shall endeavor to be as clear as possible. And I shall expect letters in reply."

"Of course," she agreed so quickly that the words tumbled over each other. "Could you correct mine, and send them back with yours?"

"I shall be as sharp and harsh as possible," he assured her. "The porcupine of French tutors."

She clasped her hands together in excitement.

"I have always longed for a porcupine," she assured him. "And what of spoken practice? Might we speak exclusively in French when we chance to run into each other socially?"

He narrowed his eyes. "My primitive male brain is starting to suspect this is the first and last house call you wish me to make."

"It's not what I wish," she said honestly. She could not have dreamed up a more perfect man than him. "It's my grandmother. If she was willing to send for a license at the mere sight of a man bearing flowers—"

"All of them had their heads when I bought them," he said with a straight face. "I think their current look gives them character."

"You are the character," she said with a laugh. "If Koffi hadn't chased Grandmother away, she'd be—"

Half in love with you herself.

"—dragging us to the altar," Priscilla finished. "I don't want to give her false hope."

Nor him. Now more than ever, she wished she could explain that it was not him she was rejecting, but drudgery. She'd lived a boring, stagnant life long enough. The inheritance was her one chance at something more.

As long as they were both clear that whatever frisson they shared between them could never lead to more, surely a *friendship* could do no harm. Right?

Mr. Middleton nodded slowly. "I see."

"Is it…" Her voice trailed off.

Was it what? Fair? He was giving and she was taking. What made her think he had any wish to prolong a doomed friendship?

"*C'est le destin,*" he said, and swept an elegant bow. "*Je m'appelle* Thaddeus. *Et vous?*"

"Priscilla," she stammered, then realized she'd squandered her first chance to practice French with a true partner. She started again. "*Je m'appelle* Priscilla. *Et je suis… er… enchantée.*"

"*Cherche les signes,*" he said with a crooked

smile, then walked to the door. "Goodbye, Koffi. *Au revoir,* Priscilla."

"Goodbye, my love!" Koffi squawked. "¡Adios, mi amor!"

Priscilla slumped against the closest wall and muttered, "*Merde.*"

CHAPTER 7

*P*riscilla stalked the perimeter of the Everett ballroom with restless energy. She wanted to be at home, in case Thaddeus sent another letter. She wanted to be *here*, in case Thaddeus was, too. She wanted…

She wanted *Thaddeus*, blast it all.

Even the usual amusement of playing the points game had paled in comparison. In the week since his visit, she hadn't so much as glimpsed him… but their two letters a day had turned to three, then to four. She was forced to admit her eagerness for each one was just as much because they were from *him* as because of French.

"Ninnyhammer," she muttered to herself.

So what if her halting sentences and his po-etic eloquence had quickly become the deepest conversations she'd ever held with another per-son? Letters were not the point. She could dash off missives for the rest of her life, if she wished.

The goal was adventuring with Papa and Grand-father, and the *means* to that goal was fluency.

Not that Priscilla doubted their sincerity in welcoming her aboard after her twenty-fifth birthday. They might not remember to come home to fetch her, but wasn't that what the inheritance was for?

Once she found them, however; once she joined their caravan in Africa with as much zeal and doggedness as any man; once she displayed her willingness to cook or clean or tend camels and horses; once she not only proved herself an asset at camp but also her ability to communicate as easily in French as well as English...

Why, she'd be positively indispensable, wouldn't she? Her grasp of Baoulé was limited, granted, but she'd pick it up while she was there, garnering Papa and Grandfather's admiration and respect in the process... and finally become non-leave-behind-able.

The image sent her heart pounding with the familiar rush of hope and excitement. She was almost there. She just had to stay away from the altar—and from scandal—for a little while longer.

"Miss Weatherby?" The Duke of Colehaven stood before her with his hand outstretched. "Never say you've forgotten our dance."

"Woolgathering," she admitted, and placed her hand in his. "I've been looking forward to this all evening."

Normally, Priscilla wouldn't be caught dead

in the arms of a titled gentleman. Romantic interest from a duke would spur romantic interest in all the others, and romance was the last thing she needed.

The Duke of Colehaven, however, was safely married. He was also the elder brother of Priscilla's friend Felicity, who had orchestrated this quadrille in order to partner with a certain earl.

Or was it a marquess? Felicity's list of admirers read like a summary of *Debrett's Peerage*. If word had got out that she was finally willing to accept an offer, gentlemen would be queuing up for miles.

"How is your parrot?" Colehaven asked.

"A joy and a terror," Priscilla answered promptly. Although few other than Thaddeus had met Koffi, Colehaven knew of his existence because of Priscilla's friendship with Felicity. "How is the Wicked Duke?"

"Wickeder by the day," Colehaven assured her. "This is our tenth anniversary, but so far I've spent much of it in Parliament." He pulled a face.

Priscilla schooled her features into an appropriately sympathetic look. "Less beer for you?"

"More, actually." His grin was contagious. "Diana and I are installing a brewing room at home. I can't wait to taste what we come up with. She knows just as much about ale as I do."

Twenty points to the duke and twenty to Diana, Priscilla decided. If one *were* to leg-shackle oneself to a man equally leg-shackled to London, marrying someone as obviously devoted as the

Duke of Colehaven was the best possible outcome. She was thrilled for both her friends.

Thrilled, but not jealous. Diana and Colehaven were one couple in a million. The rest of the ballroom was filled with empty husks rushing into miserable marriages for political or societal or monetary reasons.

They either doomed themselves to a lifetime of sharing a bed and a dining table with a barnacle they longed to leave behind, or they gave up the pretense altogether and lived as strangers, taking their pleasure in the arms of a lover or anywhere else they might find it.

No, thank you. Priscilla preferred to do the leaving-behind herself.

"What do you think?" Colehaven asked, tilting his head toward his sister and her partner. "Is the marquess the one?"

If his pockets are deep enough.

Priscilla would never make such a statement aloud, of course. At least, not to Colehaven. Felicity was always open about her necessary qualifications for a suitor. Unlike Priscilla, she expected to live at a level significantly above sweaty camels and mud-splattered tents.

They were opposites in so many ways. Priscilla had never wanted for any creature comfort or physical luxury. What she hadn't had was support, encouragement, love... someone to miss her.

Felicity, on the other hand, had suffered through years without every possible physical comfort and necessity... but had never once doubted that she was needed, and loved, and important, and cherished.

"Your sister will be fine," Priscilla said softly.

The duke nodded. "I know. But I can't stop worrying. She's my sister." His brow lined with worry. "Mayhap I'll increase her dowry again."

Priscilla nodded, and pretended to understand.

The money left in trust was one of the few instances of proof her father and grandfather thought of her at all, much less placed any specific value on her.

At her come-out, when a young, wide-eyed Priscilla had asked about the size of the dowry, she'd been devastated to discover there was no dowry at all. Nothing.

Either Papa and Grandfather forgot, as Felicity tried to assure her, or they expected her to make a brilliant match through her own wiles, as Grandmother preached, or they didn't expect her to choose the bridal path at all, as Priscilla believed.

Why else would they fail to create a dowry? They were waiting for her. Counting on her. She would not let them down.

"Look," Colehaven whispered, giving a subtle nod toward another foursome on the dance floor. "See the sort of man Felicity chooses?"

Priscilla's heart stuttered and she stumbled.

The duke caught her. "Are you all right?"

"Splendid," she croaked.

Priscilla was not all right. She had just glimpsed Thaddeus Middleton.

Her lungs could no longer breathe.

She had not heard his name announced, which meant he had arrived before her.

For two long sets, she had searched for him, and he had been here this whole time. No smile. No word of greeting. Not even a polite nod from across the room.

In fact, she hadn't seen him at all until this moment, which seemed to imply he'd been otherwise occupied, somewhere out of the public eye.

Perhaps with the woman currently simpering in his arms.

"Are you certain you're all right?" Colehaven asked again.

Priscilla nodded jerkily. "Capital."

Besides, what had she expected? She'd told Thaddeus that she was uninterested in marriage; he was a charming bachelor who *was* interested in marriage...

It was just a matter of time before he found what he was looking for and abandoned his silly epistolary friendship with Priscilla.

As soon as the music drew to a close, she dipped the requisite curtsy to Colehaven and fled the dance floor.

She was finished with ballrooms, finished watching Thaddeus dance with other women. Young, pretty, eligible women. Women that would actually marry him.

With the requisite quadrille out of the way, she could now safely retire to the library for a set or two. No one would notice her absence, and a bit of quiet solitude would allow her to regain her lost equilibrium.

Just by crossing the threshold into the silent, peaceful library, Priscilla felt her pulse slow back to normal. This was what she needed. Something to take her mind off a romance she'd known from the moment she'd seen him at Almack's that she could not have.

She strode to the bookshelves at the far side of the library. This section was furthest from the soft light of the fire, but the books on these shelves were more interesting. Three entire rows of uncut volumes on travel.

Priscilla would never presume to slice someone else's pages for reading—tempting though it might be—but must content herself instead with the maddening game of imagining everything she was missing as she leafed through.

As before, there was still only one volume dedicated to equatorial Africa. She'd all but memorized the fifty visible percent of its pages during past escapes to this same nook of the library.

She reached for the volume anyway.

"*Bonsoir*, Mademoiselle Weatherby," came a low, familiar voice.

Priscilla spun about, abandoning the travel book.

"Oh," she stammered. "Er, good evening. I mean, *bonsoir.*"

Splendid. *Incredibly* fluent. She was going to take the entire world by storm with her effortless command of riveting French conversation.

"Toutes les soirées que je passe avec vous sont belles."

Likely, Priscilla should at least attempt to parse this phrase and respond accordingly.

She could not.

The air had been sucked from the room upon his arrival. She had thought this phenomenon an ancillary effect of the stagnant air in her grand-mother's townhouse, but here in the Everetts' spacious library, Priscilla had been breathing very well until Thaddeus entered the room.

He looked like a painting come to life. Not some Roman statue or an insipid fashion plate, but a warrior disguised behind a neckcloth and tailcoat. The heat from his eyes made her tremble with desire.

She did not feel safely sequestered in the shadows of a slightly chilly private library, but rather like a young gazelle exposed on the wide plains of the Sahara desert, skin drenched in sun and sweat, her scent on the wind, her trail too obvious to hide. And yet she did not run away.

"You were dancing," she said inanely.

He stepped closer. "So were you."

There was nowhere to go. Her shoulder-blades all but touched the wide mahogany shelves behind her back, and his broad chest was little more than an arm's breadth away.

Not that she felt like running. She was more likely to use the shelves as a crutch to keep her upright.

"I didn't know you were here." Her cheeks tinged with heat. "Before I saw you dancing, I mean."

"I wasn't in the ballroom," he agreed. "Diana wanted Lady Everett to have a current list of—" He shook his head, his expression one of fond indulgence. "Never mind the proper weight of a grain bushel. How can a man possibly keep weights and measures reform in his head when his eyes are looking at you?"

"Er," Priscilla said brilliantly. "*Je ne sais pas?*"

What she *did* know was that she was ridiculously, irrationally relieved to discover Thaddeus had not been wooing some other woman, but rather had been on a mundane mission for his cousin.

Relieved and melancholy.

His obvious affection for his cousin was heartwarming... and also tied him down. Although he possessed no political obligation to the House of Lords, it seemed Thaddeus would never venture far from London or family.

She'd learned everything about everyone, to better arm herself to play the game. She used her knowledge to stand just outside the circle. Thaddeus used his to stand right in the middle.

He was a settling-down sort of man, a home-is-where-the-heart-is sort of man, a here-have-a-leg-shackle sort of man. A marriage proposal from him would be nothing more than a pretty prison. An invitation to never leave the one place she longed to escape.

He was *not* for her. And yet...

Thaddeus leaned a shoulder against the closest shelf, his warm brown gaze meeting hers. "I missed you."

"I wrote you five letters today." Poring over each word of his reply. Deducting a thousand points each time.

"It wasn't enough," he said softly. "I longed to see you. The sweetest words are the ones I witness falling from your lips."

Don't get swept away, she warned herself. Charming gentlemen reused the same thoughtless compliments with every lady they met. It meant nothing. She wasn't special.

"Today," he continued, "I learned the word *taloua*." His eyes were hot on hers. "It means 'beautiful.' Or possibly 'maiden.' To be honest, every Baoulé word reminds me of you."

To this, Priscilla had no response. Formulating coherent answers was difficult when one's heart had just swooned in one's chest.

"You're learning *Baoulé?*" she stammered.

He flashed a shy, boyish smile. "I'm not fluent, but I could try. If you wanted."

She could have laughed. Or cried.

He was *everything* she wanted. Sweet and caring, considerate and insightful, unashamed to admit he'd been thinking about her and perfectly willing to do something about it. He missed her. And told her so. Was there anything she'd yearned for more?

"You'd really learn Baoulé," she ventured, "just to write me letters?"

"That's the only practical use I see," he said with a little laugh. "It's not like I'd *go* there. Can you imagine how long the trip would take?"

"Five to six months," she said immediately. "From port to port. The rest would be by land. If you took a camel—"

"I would not take a camel," he assured her. "Keeping cat hair from black trousers is difficult enough."

"I recommend forgoing evening suits whilst astride a camel," she advised him. "I'm no valet, but I do feel camel-riding is more of a buckskin breeches activity?"

"Hmm." He affected a pose of deep concentration. "But what if I am riding the camel during the evening?"

"Then no one can see the little yellow hairs on your breeches anyway," she pointed out. "Besides, by the time you got wherever you were going, your clothes would be out of fashion anyway. Not to mention sun-faded and mud-stained."

"And that," Thaddeus said, "is the real reason I would never do it. I am a very fashionable gentleman, constantly out-fashioning everyone else, and it would wound my ego to become the sec-

ond-most fashionable gentleman because I decided to take a six-month hackney ride."

Her lips twitched. "You might be the first-
most handsome gentleman in all of London, but
that waistcoat hasn't been *à la mode* in three
seasons."

He clutched his palm to his chest with a gasp.
"A well-bred lady would never insinuate such a
horrid thing!"

"Well-bred ladies also don't ride camels," she
said with a shrug, and then paused. "That can't
possibly be true. How else could they get from
one place to another?"

"Horses," he pointed out. "Or giant marmots.
Whatever's native. Why are you so determined to
do everything on camel-back?"

"Because I've never done *anything* on camel-
back," she admitted. "Or marmot-back, now that
you mention it. But I'll let you go first with the
marmot."

"I'm not going at all," he reminded her with a
little shudder. "Think of all I would have to give
up. What if Gunter's has no tea shops in Africa?"

"What if there are countless treats a hundred
times better?" she countered. "Don't you agree it
would be amazing to hop on a ship and explore
the four corners of the world for the rest of your
life?"

"No?" His expression was comical. "Have you
ever *tasted* quinine?"

She blinked. "Have you?"

He waved this away. "It *sounds* like something

that would taste dreadful. I'll stick to the ales at the Wicked Duke, if you please."

She bit her lip. "Would you really be content never to leave England?"

"I *have* left," he admitted. "As soon as the war was over, I took an extended trip to the Continent. France is a stone's throw away. I would return in a heartbeat."

A pleasant rush of surprise took her. "You do like to travel?"

"I love people," he reminded her. "Other countries are full of walking biographies. If I had the means, I'd spend a month on the Continent every year."

If I had the means. Therein lay the rub.

He was almost perfect. He did like adventure. But he wasn't willing to go further than the Continent, and didn't even have enough blunt to do that much. Add in the expense of a wife, and Thaddeus Middleton would be spending the rest of his life in England whether he wished to or not.

"What about you?" he asked. "Would you really give up having roots and a place to call home?"

"It's what I've always wanted," she said softly. A life of excitement and adventure. It was the driving force behind everything she did. "Not everyone has the same dreams, and that's a good thing. Your biographies must illustrate that. Differences are what make people interesting."

"True enough," he conceded, his eyes losing

focus. "If everyone was the same, I wouldn't have filled up half as many journals with..." He cleared his throat and turned toward the shelves. "What were you in here looking for?"

"Just a moment." She folded her arms beneath her breasts and stared at him in fascination. "You don't just *read* biographies... you write them?"

"No," he said quickly. "I take notes. Copious notes. For future biographies that I also definitely won't write. It's very boring. Let's go back to talking about quinine. Malaria is such a charming subject. Are you planning to contract scurvy first? It *is* a long boat ride over."

"You write," she said in wonder. "I would love to read something you wrote."

"You read my words every day," he reminded her. "I have kept you faithfully up-to-the-minute on the goings-on at Chez Middleton."

"And you're brilliant at it," she told him. "Even in French, I can picture everything just as you describe and giggle over the amusing bits even on second or third reading."

He stared at her, startled. "You reread my letters?"

"Endlessly." She gave him a lopsided smile. "Your words could only be sweeter if I witnessed them fall from your lips."

"That's not all my lips can do, *ma très chère*," he said with an exaggerated swagger, clearly meant to break the spell of the moment.

But the magic only intensified, pulling them closer together.

"Show me," she said, daring to place her fingertips against the heat of his lapels. "What can those beautiful lips do?"

He answered with his body, rather than with words, angling his head closer, slowly, allowing her time to laugh and pull away and claim it had all been a game.

But she was no longer playing for points. She wasn't playing at all. If she was about to have her first kiss, she wanted it to be him.

As his lips brushed hers, she felt herself falling back toward the bookshelves.

He caught her and pressed her to him, aligning their bodies indecently in the best possible way.

His lips were warm and firm and patient. But Priscilla didn't want to wait. She wanted it all. No holding back. When she left, there would be no more kisses. But for now, could it not be an innocent indulgence like the letters they shared?

Perhaps not *completely* innocent, she allowed as she sank her fingers into the wild curls at his nape. One of his hands cupped her head, the other supported the small of her back. But she wasn't going anywhere. Not yet.

He pulled his mouth from hers just long enough to ask, "What are your intentions with me, mademoiselle?"

"Carnal and dishonorable," she answered, sliding her bosom against him as she rose up to bring her mouth next to his. "I'm a heartless rake who promises nothing and wants everything."

His mouth curved into a wicked smile brimming with temptation. "Then let me give it to you."

The next time he brushed his parted lips against hers, she parted hers as well. He tasted her mouth, her tongue, coaxing, giving, taking. If it weren't for his arm about her waist and her hands twined about his neck, she could have swooned from the delectable sensations.

Except, no—she was far from swooning. With her heart galloping and her passions aflame, she had never felt more alive. *This* was life. *This* was adventure. Exploring the shape of his mouth, the taste of his tongue, the hardness of his muscles, the softness of his hair.

This wasn't just a kiss. This was *Thaddeus*. She could no longer deny her feelings, if only to herself. Magic like this was something that could only be built together.

He was taking her to new peaks, showing her new climes. She had not known that a trail of kisses along the curve of her neck could be felt all the way to her core. She had not known about the sensitive spot behind the shell of her ear, or how the brush of his thumb against the side of her ribs would cause her nipples to—

"—library is just up ahead," came a shrill voice from the corridor.

They flew apart, panting, their bodies still yearning to cleave back together.

Priscilla snatched the book on Africa off the shelf and hugged it to her breathless bosom.

"Go," she whispered. "Before we're seen together."

He hesitated, then lifted a hand to her cheek. "If we *were* caught, I would have no problem with—"

"I would," she interrupted, pulling away from his touch. "It can't be more than kisses. I'm sorry."

CHAPTER 8

It can't be more than kisses.

Thad was trying very hard to return coherent greetings to all the friends he passed as he made his way through the Vauxhall pleasure gardens, but all he could think of were the last words Priscilla had spoken.

Kisses. Plural. That was a positive sign, was it not?

She had not said, "We'll never repeat this" or "What was I thinking?" but rather seemed to imply that as long as he could content himself with clandestine kisses, Thad could have as many of them as he liked.

He very much liked. He could think of nothing else in the days since the Everett ball.

Their letters had not slowed in number, but of course made no mention of how it had felt to finally find themselves in each other's arms. That was not the sort of missive Priscilla would wish intercepted by her grandmother, and if Thad were honest, scandal was not his first preference on how to visit the altar.

When he wed, it would be to a woman who chose him, not one who was forced to settle for him. Perhaps that meant Priscilla wasn't the one.

He felt more entwined with her with each exchanged letter. Watching her sail off for Africa would wrench a heart-sized hole in his chest. But he would not force her to pretend something she did not feel. To accept a life she did not want. He would rather be lonely forever than ruin two lives with one marriage.

So, yes. He could console himself with kisses. Hot, sweet, drugging kisses. The sort of kisses that made a man wish he did long for scurvy on the high seas or whatever else it took to keep her hands about his neck and her soft curves locked tight against him.

"Missed you at the Wicked Duke this week, old chap." A vicar clapped Thad on the shoulder. "Weren't you meant to debate with Barrett?"

Was he?

"Next time," Thad said vaguely.

He could not recall having promised such a thing. For the past fortnight, he'd only accepted invitations if there was a chance of Priscilla being in attendance. Only women with little or no reputation stepped foot in the tavern.

Then again, Priscilla was far from the usual missish debutante. She was just as likely to burst into the Wicked Duke on the back of a camel as anything else. Perhaps he should give up on plea-sure gardens at once, and see if she—

"Middleton," called another friend. "Going to Tattersall's tomorrow to see the new racehorses?"

"Doubtful," he called back.

Unlike the Wicked Duke, Tattersall's didn't allow women at all, regardless of how tattered the reputation. He would stick to the places Priscilla was known to frequent.

Tonight, in any case, he had promised his cousin Diana to find her near the supper-boxes. The sun was setting, which meant she and her husband would be finishing their meal.

Thad did not hurry. The Colehavens would stay for the orchestra, and besides, the evening was too fine for barreling through it with one's head pointed at the ground.

Vauxhall was his favorite pleasure garden, and one of the most crowded places in London. He loved to daydream about all the fascinating bi-ographies passing by on all sides. Tightrope walkers, pie men, groundskeepers, flautists, royal footmen. He could write about someone new every day of the week without having to leave the park.

The indefatigable energy of the flower girls. A secret smile between a milkmaid and a vegetable vendor. The trysts unfolding in the infamous Dark Walk as the sun slipped out of sight.

If it weren't for his social commitment with Diana, Thad would be just as happy to perch upon a bench with his pencil and a journal and scribble notes for the rest of the night.

Happier yet if he could catch a glimpse of Priscilla...

Try as he might, he could not keep her out of his mind for more than a moment. Their kiss was unforgettable, their letters grew funnier and more meaningful and intimate every time, and yet he *knew* better than to hope for a fairy-tale with her.

"Happy ever after" didn't come to those who wished for it. It depended on fate, and theirs did not seem to be intertwined.

It hadn't stopped him from dedicating an entire journal to her, of course. He captured every word he could remember, every feeling, every story. Even the ones she didn't quite tell.

Her father and grandfather had chosen adventure over the women who loved them. Her mother had left in another way. Her grandmother was just as distant, despite never leaving home. Thad did not blame her for wanting different; for wanting *better*.

That these actions did not diminish Priscilla's love for her family spoke all the more highly of her. Her love was pure and unconditional. Who could fail to admire a woman who could love like that?

"Middleton!" The Duke of Eastleigh and his new wife paused to greet him. "Please tell me you're not avoiding the Wicked Duke because of

Marsh's ridiculous tiff over the new porter. He claims his is better than Cole's."

The tavern's head brewer was always in a tiff over something. It had never stopped Thad from enjoying the libations.

"I've been busy," he said, and changed the subject. "How are the plans for the circulating library?"

The duke and duchess exchanged a loving look. "We are busily accumulating the finest inventory," Eastleigh answered.

Thad tried very hard not to be envious Eastleigh had beaten the odds and been reunited with his lost love. Could destiny be any more romantic than that?

He knew what that meant, of course.

Not Priscilla.

The worst possible choice would be someone who wanted something else, someone with one foot out the door, someone with better options.

His hands turned clammy at the familiar dread. The spark might be there, but so was the fear of making the same mistake his father had. The last thing Thad wanted was to fall in love with someone who would never be pleased she had married him... or never marry him at all.

He would be destroyed if he married the girl he adored only for her to fall out of love because he couldn't be what she needed. That was not a road he was willing to travel. He tightened his jaw with determination.

For the right woman, he *would* be the best option. That was what would make her The One and lift her above any other. There would never be any question of having settled for less than what they wanted. No chance of love souring into resentment. Just happy ever after.

"Thad!" A familiar head popped out from one of the supper-boxes and motioned him over.

Grinning, he made his way toward his cousin. "Diana!"

"Your Grace, the Duchess of Colehaven," she corrected with a saucy grin. "That's how titles work."

He widened his eyes. "I don't know about titles, madam. I haven't got one of my own."

She rapped his knuckles with her fan. "That'll be 'Your Grace' to you, sir."

"Ow!" He pretended to shake the pain from his fingers. "Why are you carrying a fan? It's March. At *night*."

"We arrived before sunset," she answered primly. "And besides, it's unseasonably warm. Can you recall such a clear night?"

He glanced up at the stars spanning the heavens and had to admit it was indeed an exceptional night.

"How was supper?" he asked.

Her eyes brightened. "For the first course, footmen brought out heavy trays filled with—"

But Thad was no longer paying attention. He had just caught sight of two young ladies making their way straight toward them. One was Lady

Felicity, the Duke of Colehaven's younger sister. The other was...

Priscilla.

She was far more beautiful than any flower the pleasure gardens had on display. It wasn't the soft curls of her brown hair or the scarlet pelisse over a midnight blue gown, but the woman herself. Stubborn and confident and clever. Nothing else could steal his breath like the merest glimpse of her.

"If you like her," Diana said with dry amusement, "then you ought to put a ring on her."

"What?" he stammered, suddenly aware that he'd cut her off mid-sentence to stare slack-jawed at one of her friends. "I don't like anything. I'm very unlikeable. A miser of likes."

"False. You had an expression usually reserved for puppies and kittens," Diana said. "It was the *ahhh* face. The I-would-snuggle-with-that face. The I-want-it-in-my-arms-right-now face. And you were making it at... Priscilla."

"What?" he spluttered. "Priscilla? I've never thought of her as anything other—"

But Diana was already doubled over with laughter. "Deny it *now*, cousin. I dare you. You were making Priscilla the *ahhh* face. The *ohh* face. The—"

"When I want your opinion," he growled under his breath. "I'll tell you."

"No sparks?" she asked innocently.

"Several sparks," he admitted. "But she wants to be the heroine of a different story." He looked away. "It doesn't matter what I want, if she doesn't want it, too."

"Talk to her," Diana suggested. "Tell her you like her at least as much as your kitten."

"I'm glad you're Colehaven's problem now," he informed her, and strode toward Priscilla.

When she caught sight of him, her expression melted suspiciously close to an *ahhh* face before she shuttered all emotion away and whispered something into the ear of her companion.

Felicity immediately made a hard turn in the direction of the Colehavens' supper-box.

Priscilla remained on the far side of the open area, buffeted by streams of passers-by heading to and from the manicured walks.

He was there in ten strides.

"Not here," she hissed before he could so much as greet her.

She disappeared behind a hedgerow, leaving him no choice but to follow behind.

"Where are we going?" he whispered.

"We can't be seen displaying affection publicly," she hissed back.

He was thrilled to hear her admit that they shared more than sparks between them, and even more thrilled at the implication that she fully intended to be right back in his arms.

She pulled him into the labyrinthine shadows of the Dark Walk and turned to face him.

Probably turned to face him. He could see nothing but her outline.

"I missed you," he said to the darkness.

Two soft hands slid into his. "I missed you, too."

His heart leapt for joy. His brain knew better. He was going to hate it when she left.

"Let me write a biography about you," he said impulsively.

It would give them a reason to spend more time together. And it would be something to remember her by when she was gone.

Her warm chuckle tickled him through the darkness. "There's nothing to write. Wait until I'm a famous adventurer."

But they both knew that would never happen. Once she left, she would be gone for good.

"I should start now," he insisted. "There's always a Part One, before the famous adventurer becomes famous. Later, you'll be too hard to track down. All my information will come from snippets I collect from the newspapers."

Silence stretched between them. Thad did not know if the picture he'd painted brought her joy or sorrow.

"All right," she said at last. "And when you're a famous biographer, I'll be the one who can tell my fellow adventurers, 'C'est mon cher Thaddeus! Ah, I knew him when.'"

His visceral reaction to *that* image was definitely bittersweet. Was there no hope for something more?

He dropped his hands from hers and slid his fingers to cup her face instead.

"What are you doing?" she asked breathlessly.

He lowered his head toward hers. "Waiting for a sign."

Just as his lips touched hers, the orchestra sprang into song, filling the air all around them with a crescendo of music and beauty.

Thad barely heard it. Priscilla's mouth was beneath his, and her hands were in his hair. He could think of nothing but holding her a little longer, cherishing her warmth, committing each moment to memory.

With each press of her body against his, each touch of their tongues, each leap in his racing pulse, he fell into her and she into him until it felt like nothing else existed but their kiss.

He told her with each kiss, each caress, exactly how he felt. It wasn't love, he assured himself desperately. Not yet. But the emotion was perilously close. He was either teetering on the brink of his greatest adventure or the precipice of despair.

He would not be in Part Two of her story, but he damn well was going to be more than a footnote in Part One. Whether she crossed the endless sea or trudged across an African desert, every time the world she'd left behind fluttered to mind, he wanted it to be *this* moment, *this* kiss, *this* embrace. The man whose arms wrapped so tight about her.

And as his hungry mouth covered hers once more, the heavens filled with fireworks.

CHAPTER 9

$\mathcal{T}$he colorful fireworks exploding overhead matched the syncopated intensity of Priscilla's racing heart. She clung to Thaddeus, the seclusion of the private walks leaving her free to kiss him to her heart's content.

But was there any achievable quantity of kisses that could ever be enough?

She didn't know, and right now she didn't care. The only things that mattered were the feel of his strong arms and the heat of his intoxicating kisses.

It was more than the warmth of his skin, the sturdy strength of him beneath her hands. When she was with him, she felt like the center of his world. His attention never wavered, his gaze never faltered, his embrace always ready and waiting to receive her.

No one could be more steadfast than Thad-

ERICA RIDLEY

deus, yet to depend on him, to rely on his presence was a storm too dangerous to weather. She could truly count on no one but herself. Life had taught her this truth again and again. And yet, it was so tempting to trust, to surrender, to wish.

They had been gone too long already. She knew it; he likely did too. And yet the specter of having to exit his embrace made her cling to him all the more.

Their first kiss had been magical, but this one was even better. It was *familiar*. Safe and comforting, and at the same time reckless and freeing. This was the kiss of two people who had walked away only to come back for more.

She would never get enough of a kiss as powerful as that.

As long as they took care not to make spectacles of themselves publicly, did they truly need to stop? They could share moments like this privately... if temporarily.

Reality threatened to intrude on the romance of the moment, but Priscilla shoved it away. He missed her. He wanted her. She was always welcome in his arms. The heady sensation was far too redeeming and flattering to turn away.

Worse, she felt the same. The days without him, the excruciating hours between each new letter, now seemed a torture too devious to withstand. She missed him, blast it all. She wanted him and he knew it. She wouldn't let it go further. She couldn't allow herself to *need* him.

And yet, that was exactly how it felt. Out here in the shadows, her lips pressed to his as the wind unraveled her hair and her heart beat against his.

With him, she felt more at home than she ever did in the house she grew up in. Those walls were cold; his arms were warm. Those windows were shuttered; his heart was wide open. Those rooms were still and unchanging. He was passion and movement and color and excitement and adventure.

Soon, she would no longer be of marriageable age. A spinster. Not a has-been, but a never-was. Every season that slipped by, every waltz left undanced, every minute spent in the background was another brick in that wall.

That was the game. The goal. Disreputable lady explorer, and proud of it. A single fare to adventure. It's what she'd always wanted. What she was so close to having. Yet he made her wish she could leave an open door.

She could *not* let herself fall in love. No matter how good he felt. No matter how desperately her body longed to join with his. She had already said goodbye to too many people she loved. She would not survive adding another name to the list.

Trembling, she forced herself to break the kiss. She expected him to ask why.

If she told the truth about her inheritance, her confession would automatically break the terms.

But Thaddeus had proven himself trustworthy. There was no doubt he could keep a secret. From the first, she'd warned him whatever they had between them was temporary, but she was starting to feel he deserved to know the full reason why.

He did not ask.

Nor did he force her back into his arms, or try to kiss her again.

Instead, he pressed his lips to her forehead. "You should go back while we're still wise enough to walk away."

Priscilla was not at all certain much of her willpower remained, but she rose to press her lips to his one last time and then hurried back to the harsh light of reality.

It didn't help dispel the magic of his kiss.

She could still feel it on her lips, hours later, when the coachman delivered her and her maids back to the townhouse. Tonight, she would go straight to bed and dream about Thaddeus and an alternate world where they could both have everything they wanted—including each other.

"Come hither!" snapped a sharp voice before she made it to the stairs.

Priscilla pivoted toward the front parlor in surprise. Grandmother was always asleep at this hour.

She stepped into the lifeless drawing room, marveling that its shrouded interior seemed much bleaker than the Dark Walk. She hoped no unwelcome surprises awaited within.

"Yes, Grandmother?"

"Where were you?" her grandmother demanded.

In a man's arms.

On the Dark Walk.

Kissing.

"At Vauxhall," she said. "With Lady Felicity. I told you earlier."

"And I told you to stop playing games and find a husband," Grandmother snapped. "If you have to trap a man to get him, do it."

Priscilla's mouth fell open. "You can't possibly mean—"

"It worked for me," Grandmother said flatly.

Did it? Priscilla wanted to ask as she stabbed the fire iron into the coals to coax out more light.

"A package arrived." Grandmother motioned a brown-paper parcel on the tea table. "For you. Is it from Mr. Middleton?"

Priscilla didn't answer. Grandmother would have worked that much out on her own, either from the package itself, the footman who brought it, or the simple fact that this house had never received a letter from any man but Thaddeus.

Grandmother sniffed. "Marry him."

"No." Priscilla spun around to face her. "No husband. Why should I? You aren't happy, and neither was Mother."

"Your mother was too weak." Grandmother made a face, her tone disparaging. "I knew it the day my son married her. I brought you up to be made of sterner stuff. Thicker skin."

"You *didn't* bring me up," Priscilla burst out. "You stayed in this room for three-and-twenty years while I was left to grow up in another. And Mother wasn't 'weak.' She was *sad*. Your son abandoned her within a year of their wedding day—"

"She knew who and what he was when she married him," Grandmother said. "We all make our choices."

"—and then she died of a broken heart." Priscilla's hands curled into fists.

"Died by her own hand," Grandmother spat. "I told you. She was weak."

Priscilla's lungs struggled for air. No one had ever said those words to her before, but even at nine she'd known the truth.

She supposed she *was* made of sterner stuff, had been forced to be by necessity, or else be broken-hearted herself that leaving a frightened little girl behind hadn't been a good enough reason for her mother to want to live.

"Strong," she whispered. "I'm strong."

"You're slow," Grandmother corrected. "I expected you married by now."

"With what wiles?" Priscilla burst out. "I have no title, no dowry… I had to teach myself to read—"

"Men don't want a clever woman," Grandmother retorted. "They want her to be docile.

They want regal. They want a woman who knows her place."

"I don't know mine," Priscilla said, chin held high, "because I don't intend to have one. I'll spend the rest of my life off on adventure, waking each morn to a day full of wonder and surprises—"

"You hate wonder and surprises," Grandmother said, her tone disparaging. "You claim to like the idea of the unknown, but have gone to great lengths to know and predict every single element in your environment."

Priscilla's breath tangled in her throat and she wrapped her arms about her chest. "I…"

"Even your wretched parrot can quote Debrett's," Grandmother continued. "You're at Almack's every Wednesday—"

"It's the Marriage Mart," Priscilla protested.

"You're not looking for a husband," Grandmother pointed out. "You're attending the most predictable event in all of London. And where were you tonight?"

"Vauxhall," Priscilla repeated. "And it was very, very surprising."

"I doubt that," Grandmother said with disdain. "They post upcoming events on every wall in London—"

"You've never even left home! How would you know?"

"You bring the bills home," Grandmother said with satisfaction. "The maids have told me. Every bill, every ticket, clippings from every newspaper—"

Priscilla dug her fingernails into her palms and ground her teeth together. She could not admit that she'd been hoarding snippets of her life in an album meant for her Father.

When he came back and asked what she had been up to, he would be able to leaf through her life page by page. See everything he had missed. And then they would close that book and leave it behind because the rest of her life was something they'd share together.

"Don't tell me," Grandmother said in disgust.

Priscilla's cheeks flushed. Her face had given her away.

"He's coming back," she said firmly. "And even if he doesn't, I'm still going."

Her new life, her exciting, fabulous, adventurous life, was waiting for her. She just had to get there.

"He's not coming back," Grandmother said flatly.

"He *is*," Priscilla said. "They both are. They promised."

Mother and Grandmother had both been perfect as a portrait, and they had been left behind. Priscilla had been a curious, exuberant child, and she had been left behind. But that was then. Things were different. She wasn't a baby anymore.

The thought that Papa and Grandfather *weren't* waiting for her, *weren't* hoping to see her, *weren't* anxiously awaiting her arrival was too awful to consider.

But even if Grandmother was right, it didn't matter. Priscilla was an adult. Once her inheritance was in hand, she wouldn't need anyone. She could become an intrepid adventurer with or without her father and grandfather.

Once they saw her bravery and mettle, *they* would be the ones who were sorry they'd ever left her behind.

"What do you have that they want?" Grandmother asked with a sigh.

Perhaps very little. But at the least, she would not be a cross to bear.

She'd been managing her pin money since she started receiving it at fifteen. The accounts at the linen-drapers and other shops were in Grandfather's name, and she supposed her annual fifty guinea allowance was meant for pleasures and fripperies. It was twice what the lead housekeeper earned and equal to the butler, but far more than Priscilla required.

Instead, she'd been saving half of her allowance every year. It was now up to two hundred pounds—about half what she'd earn per year from the interest on her trust. Not riches, although she believed Papa and Grandfather would be proud of her resourcefulness.

But she didn't do it for them. Those two hundred pounds had been set aside to send letters and gifts home to Grandmother, once Priscilla finally could set out for her real life.

"You think too hard," Grandmother said as if there could be no worse flaw. "You concentrate, concentrate, concentrate, but on all the wrong things."

Priscilla shook her head. Grandmother didn't know her. Never had.

And yet Priscilla could not deny a niggling worm of truth in the accusation. She longed to believe she was an open, happy-go-lucky wild thing who couldn't wait to break out of the strictures of society.

Truth was, she excelled at its game. So much so, she'd woven an even more intricate game on top, just to have more rules.

Minus a thousand points, she told herself sourly.

"Your father and your grandfather are never coming back," Grandmother said, without heat this time. "They don't think about us. It's time you think for yourself."

Priscilla *had* been thinking. Thinking was the only thing she could do, for most of her long, lonely life. Sit in her room and think-think-think about what she would do and where she would go the moment she was free of it.

But Grandmother was all she had left, and Priscilla didn't want to argue.

"Have a good night, Grandmother."

Priscilla plucked the brown-paper parcel from the tea table and swept from the parlor without waiting for a response.

Experience told her it would not have been forthcoming.

She stalked to her bedchamber and sat on the first stool with stiff legs. Hands shaking, she pushed the twine off the corners and unwrapped the package. A wistful smile touched her lips. Thaddeus understood her more than any other.

Two travel books on Africa. Three different maps. And a small, scuffed journal.

Frowning, she lifted the journal and opened it to the first page:

Miss Priscilla Weatherby,
Lady Adventurer

(Working draft)

She slammed the book closed and pressed it to her pounding chest.

He wasn't *going* to write a biography about her. He'd already started. It was right here in her hands.

She opened it back up, but the pages were impossible to read with the blurring of the words. She swiped at her eyes with her fist and focused on the first sentence. She was good at focusing. Thaddeus had done this.

For her.

When she reached the last page, her tears were gone but the hole in her chest had grown larger.

He was extraordinarily talented. Observant, insightful, witty. He made her seem strong and sure, fresh and fascinating. This, despite a life of precisely nothing. He would be a phenomenal biographer. A household name.

And he was obsessed with her... for now.

No muse lasted forever. What would happen when someone or something better came along? Because it always, always did. If her family had taught her anything, it was that love was irrelevant. The shinier object was the one men chased. No matter how much they'd once loved the jewel they left behind.

Maybe "men" weren't the problem. Maybe it was Priscilla who was leave-behind-able. A flash in the pan; exciting for a moment and then just as quickly forgotten. Not good enough to want to keep around forever.

Priscilla pushed the journal aside and went to release her parrot from his cage.

She didn't need a man. She needed adventure. She had herself, and she had Koffi.

"Tea and cake?" he said hopefully.

She fumbled for the snuff box and gave him a treat. He deserved it.

Even if no one came for her, the two of them were going anyway. Priscilla had made a promise. Others might break theirs, but she did not.

She held out a finger for him to perch on.

"Don't worry," she told him. "If you leave me when we get there, I promise not to cry."

He ignored her finger and flew high overhead where she could not reach him.

"Goodbye,   my   love!"   he   squawked. "Goodbye!"

She closed the snuff box and picked up her stack of maps and travel journals. If even Koffi was ready to leave... She should prepare herself for that day, too.

CHAPTER 10

*T*he moment he'd sent the parcel, Thad regretted allowing his manuscript out of his sight. It wasn't ready. *He* wasn't ready. Perhaps he never would be. Why, oh why, had he sent that package? Of all the dunderheaded gifts a man could give a woman…

He had spent the night far too tense and jittery to do anything so calm as *sleep*.

The morning had not fared any better. Five o'clock in the morning was far too early for house calls, and dawn two hours later wasn't much of an improvement.

Breakfast? How could he? His stomach was too busy doing somersaults to welcome toast or even tea. And still the hands of the clock moved with excruciating languor. Inch by inch. Tick by tock. He *had* to get that manuscript back.

Perhaps she hadn't read it yet.

That was the one thought that helped him survive the horrible not-knowing.

Biographies were his passion, not hers. She loved adventure. She wanted to go to Africa. Surely she'd spent the night hunched over a very practical guidebook to the western equatorial states, rather than waste time browsing a dog-eared journal's handwritten twaddle.

Eight o'clock, nine o'clock, ten. Ten and one minute. What imbecile had decreed morning calls could only be placed from eleven to three, and preferably in the afternoon? Did society not understand the definition of "morning?"

That was it. He was going now. By the time he rounded his carriage and drove from Jermyn Street to Grosvenor Square, the clock would be at least... ten-fifteen. Close enough.

What he needed was a distraction. Something so cute and cuddly and irresistible, no one would even notice him shoving his manuscript inside his jacket and running off.

Thus decided, he gathered Wednesday into her basket and hurried down the stairs to the street below.

At this hour, the streets weren't crowded. The mile from his home to Priscilla's sailed by in a trice. Before his bay could even come to a proper stop, Thad was already leaping out of the carriage.

To his surprise, not one but two footmen rushed out to greet him, relieving him of his horse and gig as if disheveled young men with shaking hands and wild bloodshot eyes always dropped by Mayfair at this ungodly hour of the morning.

This had to be the grandmother's doing, he realized. She had not been subtle in her desire for a marital outcome.

Right now, all Thad wanted to see was his manuscript.

He raised his hand toward the knocker.

The butler flung open the door. "Mr. Middleton, right this way if you please."

Thad hadn't given his card. Or mentioned which Weatherby woman he was hoping to see. He hoped he hadn't just walked into a trap.

When he entered the parlor, it looked much the same as the last time he'd seen it. Which was to say, little was visible at all. Heavy curtains blocked every trace of the early spring sunshine, and a sullen, listless fire did little to brighten the heavy interior.

"Grandmother," Priscilla was saying, as she tucked a stray tendril behind her ear. "I know you worry about me. I worry about you, too. I promise I won't forget you."

"You forget yourself," Mrs. Weatherby snapped. "A young lady's duty is to wed."

Both of them jerked startled faces toward Thad at his unexpected arrival.

"Er," he said, and made as elegant a leg as possible, given the oversized basket hanging from one arm.

"I suppose he's here to see your parrot." Mrs.

Weatherby sniffed as if this tendency alone was enough to no longer make him suitor material.

"Actually," he began, but it was already too late.

Mrs. Weatherby pushed herself out of her chair, shoved past her granddaughter, and left the parlor completely.

"She must… really hate your parrot," Thad ventured.

"It's not Koffi," Priscilla said with a sigh. "She's still hoping you'll become overset by male passion, ravish me on the parlor floor, and be forced to make an honest woman of me."

"I do feel the stirrings of unbridled male passion," he said gravely.

Priscilla arched a brow.

"And… that *is* a nice carpet," he continued as if weighing his options.

A laugh burst from her as she met him in the center of the parlor. "Why are you here?"

"To fetch my journal," he said at once. "It's mine. And a mistake. I didn't mean to send it. It's just a draft. It needs polishing. Possibly by being tossed into a fire. I even brought ammunition in case we need to work out a trade. It never should have—"

She threw her arms about him and silenced him with a kiss.

"You daft man," she said when she paused for breath. "Your talent is astonishing. I *loved* your manuscript. It's delightful and flattering and makes even my life sound riveting. You're going to be the most famous biographer England has ever seen."

"I don't know if I can handle anyone else reading my work," he groaned.

"First," she said with a laugh, "that's what publishing *is*. Second, why are you writing biographies, if not to share your wonderful stories with the world?"

"Distemper?" he guessed. "Sometimes when I'm gassy, the most absurd fancies come to mind—"

"Thaddeus," she interrupted, her eyes warm and sincere. "You have talent. You should use it. What are you waiting for?"

"Fate?" He lifted his palms. That was what he was always waiting on. Destiny to ride in on a pale horse and sweep him into his future.

"You are the one who determines your fate," she said firmly.

"Actually," he explained, "that's the opposite of what 'fate' means—"

"Fate isn't life," she interrupted, her gaze intense. "Fate is waiting around for the future to come to you, rather than going out and making it happen. Fate is in the palm of your hands. Your very lovely, talented hands."

"Talented in many ways," he assured her. "Would you believe I can tie a neckcloth without aid of a valet? Perhaps instead of being a biographer, I could become a professional cravat knotter, traveling from coast to coast to assist less dexterous gentlemen in—"

"Actually," she said, her eyes bright and intense, "with your love for meeting new people, I'm surprised your first love isn't travel. The world must be full of stories you could tell."

"It is," he agreed. "Everyone has an untold story. I could spend the rest of my life writing biographies without ever leaving London."

When her smile wobbled, he realized she hadn't been thinking of far-flung biographies, but whether there was any chance for their futures to intersect.

He didn't need to leave London, though he wouldn't mind doing so if it meant more time with her. Any holiday would be more enjoyable with Priscilla at his side.

But he wouldn't want to give up home altogether. He *liked* having a familiar place to return to. A shelf where his journals belonged, a comfortable chair before the fire, a favorite view from his balcony.

He'd been hoping to share that *with* his wife, rather than abandon it to try and keep her.

"The truth is…" he began.

He was saved from having to say what they both already knew by a sudden explosion of activity in the basket under his arm.

"What," she asked politely, "is *that?*"

"My kitten," he announced, as if even Brummell would not leave the house without a rakishly angled cat on his shoulder.

Priscilla stared at him in confusion. "Your what?"

He lifted up a corner of the lid.

A tiny, black-and-white paw poked out.

"Kitten," he repeated brightly. "I brought Wednesday to meet Saturday. Or Konan to meet Koffi. It's not every day I get to mix up languages and days of the week with one introduction."

"You brought a cat," she said slowly, "to meet my bird."

"Wednesday is a genteel cat," he assured her. "Very genteel. The genteelest."

Priscilla narrowed her eyes in warning. "If I see a single claw anywhere near my parrot..."

"No claws," Thad whispered to the basket.

The tiny paw disappeared under the lid.

"I'm warning you," Priscilla told Thad, then turned toward the corridor.

He followed her to the drawing room where Koffi lived and set his basket on the floor.

Priscilla walked not to the cage, but to the bell pull.

He blinked in surprise. It was a little late to prevent their many stolen kisses.

"Summoning a chaperone?" he asked.

"Guards," she replied. "I trust you, but I've never trusted Wednesdays."

A hesitant maid appeared in the corridor and wrung her hands just outside the threshold. "Mrs. Weatherby said..."

"To let Mr. Middleton ravish me," Priscilla concluded drily. "Duly noted. You can be dismissed if any bosoms start heaving. Meanwhile, he's about to let the cat out of the bag. If it attacks Koffi… hit Mr. Middleton with a skillet."

The maid sent her startled gaze toward Thad.

"Fair enough," he assured her. "Mostly because I see you've forgotten your skillet."

He sat down and removed the lid of the basket.

Wednesday immediately crawled up to the edge and sent delighted glances about the new foreign playground around her. She tumbled out of the basket with glee, rolling over to rub her spine against random spots on the carpet as if in search of the most comfortable corner in the room.

"It's… a kitten," the maid said.

"Her name is Wednesday," Thad said with affection. "Very fierce. The sort who might murder hapless pigeons one day. But I've spoken to her very firmly about our peace treaty with African grey parrots, and she assures me she understands."

"She'd better," Priscilla said darkly, and unlocked Koffi's cage.

He shot out at once, straight toward Wednesday, causing Thad to scramble to his feet in alarm.

Wednesday rolled onto her back and batted her little kitten paws in the air.

Startled, Koffi veered back up toward the ceiling in order to examine the newcomer from the safety of a curtain rod.

Having lost interest, Wednesday sprang upright and began prancing around the raised circular edge of the center carpet. Claws on wood. Paws on carpet. Claws on wood. Paws on carpet.

Stealthily, Koffi took another dive at the usurper.

Wednesday rolled to her back and batted a front paw in the air.

Koffi immediately changed course, choosing a different window on which to perch.

Wednesday started licking the closest bookshelf.

Priscilla looked at Thad.

He looked at her.

Koffi swooped in again, more flamboyantly this time.

Wednesday flipped over, her hindquarters propped up by a shelf and her head lolling on the floor. She batted a paw toward the air.

Koffi rose to perch on the closest window.

"I think they're... playing?" the maid ventured.

"I think so, too." Priscilla joined Thad on the settee. "Only you would have a kitten as friendly and lovable as you are."

He paused in the act of putting an arm about her shoulder.

Love.

Although she'd clearly meant to compliment his kitten in an affectionate way rather than a romantic one, Thad's feelings toward Priscilla were not nearly so sanguine.

He loved her.

Affectionate love, romantic love, let's-get-naked-now love. All of it.

He could absolutely imagine the fairy-tale. Star-crossed love and a splendid wedding. A cozy cottage and holidays abroad. A cat, a parrot, a baby or three. A house full of love and romance and laughter.

To him, it sounded perfect.

To her, it sounded like… failure. Like settling for less. Like giving up.

But what if he could convince her otherwise? He couldn't scale the Himalayas or take her diving beneath the sea, but he could offer a happy home, annual holidays, and a lifetime of love. Surely that would be just as compelling an offer as endless, grueling exploring. Wouldn't it?

"Hypothetically," he began. "If you *were* to choose between, say, eleven months a year on a boat in exchange for a few weeks' adventure, or marrying a man who—"

The maid fled the room as if her mobcap had caught fire.

"It doesn't matter what the man has," Priscilla said, "unless what he possesses is unquenchable thirst for adventure. Some people only holiday. Not me. A holiday is what you do to avoid your real life for a while. I want adventure to *be* my life. When every day is marvelous, there's no reason to want a break from it."

"But how realistic is that?" he asked gently. "I understand it's your dream, but it doesn't sound like reality. How would you afford such adventures? Who would you go with?"

Priscilla did not look like a woman who had just had the cold, hard truth splashed in her face, but rather like a woman about to deliver some cold, hard truth of her own.

"I've no dowry," she said at last. "But there is a trust I'm not supposed to talk about. If I'm unwed on my twenty-fifth birthday, I inherit a great deal of money. I can travel with my father or grandfather, or I can create an entourage of my own. For our first stop, Koffi and I are going to Africa. And then…" She gestured to shelves filled with globes and travel books. "I'll never stop moving again."

Thad could not hide his disappointment.

No dowry didn't signify. He hadn't been looking for one. But *she* was. An inheritance to do with as she pleased. And what pleased her was… leaving.

He let his arm fall back to his lap. Keeping it locked around her was nothing more than wishful thinking.

Had he feared someday falling for a woman who had a better option? Priscilla had *plenty* of better options. She didn't need him or anyone. She had adventurers in the family who would take her anywhere. And money to give her the freedom to go everywhere she wished.

That was his answer. It wasn't a question of marrying someone who would be miserable because his love wasn't enough. Thad was searching for a woman who would choose him, and Priscilla was explicitly *not* choosing him.

"When will you leave?" he asked.

Her eyes lit up. "That very day."

"When?" he insisted.

"Next year," she said. "The thirtieth of July."

There. He had his timeline. Sixteen months of knowing he was temporary and not enough. Or he could end it now. Today.

"It's why I didn't dance with you," she said softly. "At Almack's, when you asked. I wanted to very much. But the terms of the inheritance…"

She wanted to dance, but she wanted her freedom more. He could not possibly begrudge her that. Anyone would feel the same. Women, in particular, had so few options. Of course the promise of independence would have a sweeter song than a ball and chain.

"It's an incredible opportunity," he said, and meant it. "You're very fortunate."

"I know," she said. "It's everything I ever wanted." Her eyes dimmed. "Almost everything."

She was right, he realized. If she chose the life of adventure, it was all or nothing. If she married, the money from her inheritance would belong to her husband, not her. She'd lose her freedom. Her independence. Her husband could prevent her from going anywhere at all, and there would be nothing she could do about it.

Other than refuse to marry at all.

"I think I've overstayed my thirty minutes," he said and pushed to his feet.

She rose to hers as well. "Grandmother is hoping you'll break more rules than that."

But they both knew it wouldn't lead to something permanent.

"I'm sorry," she said as he gathered Wednesday into the basket.

He kissed her on the cheek. "You shouldn't be. You're making your own fate, just like you advised me to do."

She nodded, eyes sad. "And I hope you do."

"I will," he said, but didn't mean it.

Not until he was back in his carriage with the reins in his hands, basket at his side.

What if Princess Charming was the one riding off to a life of adventure and romance? His gaze flicked up toward her window. He could watch her disappear on her white steed. Or he could perhaps… join her?

He couldn't think of a perfect compromise right now, but there *had* to be something. Every minute of inaction brought him closer to the moment when it would all be too late.

Make your own fate, he told himself as he put his gig in motion.

Find a way to win her before she's lost forever.

CHAPTER 11

*T*had sat in his usual comfortable chair in its usual spot of his usual tavern and gazed out over a mug of his usual ale at all the familiar faces and lifelong friends.

Walking away from everyone and everything and every place he loved wasn't *compromise*. It was settling for less.

The irony was not lost on him.

All his life, he had been terrified of falling for someone who saw his love as second best. He'd been unwilling to force some theoretical wife to give up what she really wanted.

Now he was considering doing so himself?

There had to be another way. He wasn't against adventure. In fact, he could easily imagine exploring new horizons side-by-side with Priscilla.

Exploring, sometimes. Not all the time. He could also imagine lazy afternoons before a fire, revisiting "their walk" beneath Vauxhall's fire-

ERICA RIDLEY

works, finally having that dance they'd both wanted to say yes to, but couldn't have.

"Fresh beer?" asked a serving girl.

Thad tilted his mug to display its full, if foamless, contents.

She nodded and moved on.

Was that what Thad should do? Move on?

The idea didn't instill him with any more joy than the idea of never seeing the Wicked Duke again.

Adventure was fine. A *lifetime* of adventure... Could Priscilla really expect anyone to relinquish every other part of their lives?

The barmaid was back. She took the flat ale from his hand and replaced it with a fresh serving.

"On the house," she said with a smile.

Thad nodded.

The Wicked Duke's generosity made him want to drink his ale even less. Only valued, frequent customers received mugs of beer on the house.

He took a sip. It was delicious. He put it down.

Was that what he valued? The occasional glass of free ale because he spent so much time in the same chair in the same corner of the same place?

The Wicked Duke wasn't the end of a fairytale. It was the beginning. It was the catalyst, from which a man in love decided what the devil he intended to do about it. How he planned to make his own fate, with the woman he chose to share it with.

Priscilla made him want more than a happy ever after. She made him want it with *her*.

Thad downed his ale and rose to his feet.

If he wanted to share a life with the woman he loved, what was he doing in a tavern she couldn't even enter?

He exited into the street and blinked at the waning sun.

There was his trusty horse and gig. Arguably more stylish than the sweaty back of a camel, but was it more fun? A better story to tell the grand-children?

He untied the gig and swung up into the seat.

His horse headed for home.

Thad frowned. He'd always dreamed of sharing his home with a wife, but did it need to be the one on Jermyn Street? He was a *renter*. The townhouse wasn't even his. Did the place even matter, as long as they were together?

He didn't know precisely how they would work everything out, but the details were something a husband and wife should work out as partners.

She hadn't mentioned being amenable to looking for a compromise, but the truth of the matter, the shameful, embarrassing fact was...

He hadn't *asked*.

He'd sat there in silence, not waiting for fate to come to him but, worse, watching it walk away. They both deserved better than that.

If there was one thing that was worth risking everything for, it was love. He was in. Was she? There was only one way to find out.

He turned his horse toward Grosvenor Square.

If she said no, well… then, that was no. But at least he would have an answer. He would have *tried* to win the princess.

And if she says yes? came the niggling, insidious voice that always blocked him from trying. If she says yes, could he believe her? Believe in a future where marrying him wasn't settling for less?

And if she said no… how would he go on? Seeing her everywhere he went, counting down the days to her inheritance when he could finally put her out of his sight, if not his heart and mind.

Thad tightened his grip on the reins.

He would have to trust and risk and hope. He would be forever resentful of his own inaction if he walked away from his One True Love without even trying to make it last.

Asking her to marry him was a risk, no matter what the answer. But a "yes" didn't mean he was destined to follow in his father's footsteps into a loveless marriage.

Happy Ever After wasn't a destination, but a lifelong journey. If he married Priscilla, they would create their fate together, as partners. A team. Love wasn't a lightning strike, but the trip of a lifetime.

He handed his horse and gig to a footman. No

bluebirds and rainbows today. Night had fallen. Thad tried not to take it as a sign.

The door to the Weatherby townhouse already yawned open. This would either be the greatest moment of his life...

Or the worst.

He rolled back his shoulders. If Priscilla wanted to marry him, if she truly believed they would be happy together, then that made two of them. He'd sign any contract.

And if she could not, if happiness meant separating, if *he* was the temporary holiday...

Then Thad would be the one to walk away, and he wouldn't be back.

"This way if you please, sir," said the butler.

Thad shook his head.

The front parlor was a pretense and everyone knew it. Mrs. Weatherby had given her consent from the moment she'd glimpsed him.

The only person whose opinion mattered on the subject was Priscilla.

"Take me to Miss Weatherby, please," he said firmly.

The butler knocked on the closed door to her drawing room.

A cacophony sounded inside. "Grandmother?"

"Mr. Middleton to see you," the butler responded.

The cacophony ceased and the door swung open.

"Thaddeus?" she said in wonder. Her parrot sat on her shoulder.

The butler discreetly took his leave.

"May we speak privately?" Thad asked.

She motioned him inside and shut the door.

"Tea and cake?" squawked Koffi.

"*Shh.*" Priscilla upended the contents of what appeared to be a snuffbox onto the closest windowsill.

Koffi immediately began to dine upon the crumbs.

"I wasn't sure..." Priscilla bit her lip as she gazed up at Thad. "I'm glad to see you."

"I left things unfinished," he said. "Now I mean to finish them."

He had never been more terrified. He wondered if this was how mountain climbers felt, when they dangled from a rope halfway up a cliff. If things went well, they would become the hero of the story. But if things went badly...

"I love you," he said. There. He'd got the most frightening part out first. He ignored the racing of his heart and pushed on. "I want to share the rest of my life with you."

Her eyes flew open wide.

Thad rushed on before she could speak. This was his only chance.

"There is no fate," he said, the words coming faster. "You taught me that. I'm here not to make my own destiny, but to forge one together. You and me. Husband and wife."

She bit her lip.

"I know my limitations," he said quickly. Best to admit the worst bits first. He swallowed hard. "I'm not rich. I can't promise you endless expeditions and escapades. But I'll do my damnedest to fill our lives with as much adventure as a man in love possibly can."

Her gaze didn't leave his.

"'Happy ever after' isn't something that happens to us when we least expect it," he continued, heart beating faster. "It's a future we make for ourselves. Something we work toward together. Happiness we deserve because we're creating it for each other." He stepped forward. "You are the only adventure I want."

She opened her mouth.

He stopped her, his heart pounding. "Almost forgot the most important part."

Her gaze was unreadable.

"Miss Priscilla Weatherby..." He inhaled shakily and dropped to one knee to gaze up at her. "Will you marry me?"

CHAPTER 12

*P*riscilla's heart raced so quickly that her head grew dizzy. She hadn't thought he'd be back. But he was here. And on one knee.

He knew what he was asking, and he was asking it anyway.

She wished they could be together. But they'd never be able to keep their relationship a secret for a year and a half. And if she married him now, there went her inheritance.

More importantly… marriage was forever.

Her stomach roiled with fear. It was too hard. Too much. She loved him, but she couldn't do it. Her fingers shook. How was anyone ever certain enough about someone else to agree to give up her only opportunity for financial freedom, for independence, for a chance to pursue a dream?

Her throat locked as she replayed her own words. She *loved* him. She knew it, but had been too frightened to admit the truth even to herself. She loved him and she wanted him—and she couldn't bring herself to say yes. Now or ever.

"*Mon chéri...*" she whispered miserably.

He closed his eyes.

She wished she could close hers. It wouldn't help. The image before her was burned into her memory.

He wanted her *now*. She believed him. But it had nothing to do with tomorrow.

She was a baby when her father left. Nine, when her mother stopped getting up in the mornings. She was a little girl. She *needed* her mama. But wishes never made anything come true.

Mother had distanced herself emotionally, stopped replying verbally, stopped responding physically, and then was gone altogether. If a mother could leave, a grandfather, a father, what faith was Priscilla meant to have that any husband *she* chose would be different?

The only way to protect her heart was to keep it locked inside.

"What if I don't answer?" she said hesitantly. If she said no, she would lose him. Right now, tonight. "Can I think it over?"

"You already have." His voice was resigned, defeated. But his gaze was hot and fiery, as if the story was not over, but barely begun.

Of course she had thought it over. She'd thought of nothing but him for the past month. Every chance meeting, every hand-delivered letter, every stolen kiss and the thousands more she wished they could have stolen.

"Secret lovers" wasn't the answer he was looking for, but it was one she could give him. Not a long, drawn-out romance, but perhaps a time or two, with no other public contact that might garner attention. The slightest slip would void the terms of the trust.

Even if they could somehow hide their longing glances and midnight trysts from society, stringing things along for a year and a half would be torture for them both—and particularly unfair to him, when they both knew how it would end.

He'd said it himself: he couldn't provide the life she'd dreamed of. The life she was so close to having. The life she would have to give up, and simply *hope* that he would always take her with him, that if he left, he would always come back.

And yet, how could she say no to the man who held her heart? A life of endless adventure had once seemed like everything, and now felt like something would be missing. Like some*one* would be missing. She could fill her days with wonder after wonder, but how would she ever fill the aching hole in her chest?

"I *do* need to think," she said at last, her stomach in knots. "I thought I had thought every possible thought to think, and now my mind is all topsy-turvy again. I know what I want. I'm trying to work out how to have it. Can you... give me a little time? At least until tomorrow?"

She expected him to say no. That if she

couldn't say *yes* now, obviously no yeses were forthcoming. She expected him to be disgusted or angry or hurt.

She did not expect a smile to spread across his face, or for him to leap to his feet and swing her about the room as if they'd just won a war.

"What are you—" she tried, laughing, but he was covering her with kisses.

"It's not a no," he said, kissing her between long glances of wonder and shock. "I was so certain..."

"You thought I would say no, and you asked me anyway?" she said in surprise.

"I had to. You're my Everest, my Athens, my Baoulé," he said, his tone wry but his gaze hot and passionate. "A man can't walk away from something like that."

Priscilla wrapped her arms about him and kissed him with all the love in her heart.

"Intrepid explorer," she murmured between kisses. "Can I interest you in a different adventure?"

"What are you saying?" His tone indicated he was very, very interested.

She touched the tip of her tongue to the lobe of his ear. "You know what I'm saying."

He swept her into his arms and whirled around. "Then yes. At once. Settee? Chair? Do I finally get to ravish you on the carpet?"

"Next time," she promised. "It's unconventional, but I was thinking perhaps my bedchamber might do?"

"You *are* an unpredictable minx," he marveled and then covered her mouth with his.

She motioned toward the adjoining room without breaking the kiss.

He fumbled for the door, then backed into her bedchamber while cradling her in his arms.

"You were right," he breathed in admiration. "This carpet is far superior to the carpet in your drawing room."

"Bed," she commanded.

His gaze was suddenly serious. "You're certain?"

More than he knew. The *only* thing she knew for certain was the man in her arms loved her as much as she loved him. Whatever the morrow might bring, they could at least share one moment of passion.

"Bed," she repeated firmly. "Then everyone takes off their clothes."

"Impertinent baggage." He kissed the tip of her nose. "I like it."

She narrowed her eyes. "You're exploring too slowly."

"I'm savoring," he protested, but he lay her in the center of the bed and climbed in beside her, the front of his body flush with one side of hers.

Her heart pounded as she stared back at him. She had never been savored before. She hadn't even known that taking one's time would make the anticipation all the more erotic.

"You're beautiful," he said softly. The intensity of his gaze melted her. "I can feel when you enter a room, and from that moment, I'm lost. My eyes belong to you."

"Not true," she stammered. "I'm unremarkable by design. No one looks at me twice."

"I have you memorized." He closed his eyes and nuzzled her hair. "Your hair is as soft as I'd always imagined it to be. Thick and brown and lustrous, begging for my hands, or to be spread out on my pillow. Even when you try to hide in shadow, light from the chandelier finds you, and this soft, glorious hair shimmers and winks and tempts."

She tried to speak and couldn't. "I…"

His mouth moved from her hairline to the shell of her ear.

"I know every dip and whorl," he murmured, "because every time I see you, I imagine the things I would whisper into your ears if only I dared. Words that only lovers share."

Her pulse skipped. "Tell me now."

She could feel his smile against her skin, slow and wicked and full of promise.

"If I tell you…" he said between feathery kisses to the lobe of her ear and the sensitive pulse point just beneath. "If I tell you, you'll have all the power. I can't let you know that every time I look at you, I imagine myself inside you, with your legs clamped about me in pleasure."

"Do it." She reached for him, tried to pull his mouth to hers.

He rolled on top of her instead, propping himself on his elbows in order to place devastating kisses down the curve of her neck, the hollow beneath her shoulder, the top of her breast where it strained against her bodice.

He had not touched her anywhere intimate yet, and already her body was more alive than it had ever been. Every part of her seemed hotter, heavier, longing for his touch.

She touched him instead, allowing her fingers to explore what had previously only been exposed to her gaze. He was hot and solid, the weight of him thrilling against her.

"Naked," she gasped. "Don't we have to be naked for magic to happen?"

"There are endless ways to make magic happen," he promised, his lips brushing tantalizingly against her bosom with each word. "Mouth to breast... hip to hip... mouth even lower..."

Her head was so dizzy from his words that she didn't notice the hem of her skirt rising until a breath of cool air kissed between her thighs.

That was her last coherent thought before his mouth gave her pleasure while his fingers did the same, tormenting and teasing, promising and stroking.

"I want..." was all she managed before she dug her fingers into the sheet and exploded into a thousand fireworks.

His fingers retreated, only to be replaced by something longer, harder, thicker, rubbing against her right where he had touched, driving her mad with the desire to do it all over again.

"Together," she said, instinctively wrapping

her legs about his hips. "Promise me."

"Together," he repeated, entering gently, tantalizingly. "For as long as you want."

Forever, she answered in her mind as a short sting of pain gave way to pleasure. Their mouths sought each other as their bodies found a rhythm, a wave, a crest that kept building higher.

She'd thought she was inviting him to her bed in order to give him her virginity, but with every stroke he was taking so much more than that. He wanted her heart, but already had it. He wanted her soul, but it was his as well.

He wanted her love, her passion, her peak—

Her body began to tremble, the familiarity of the warning signs even more thrilling now that she knew what would happen.

The first time, he'd done this *to* her. Now, he was doing it *with* her. When she took, he took, too. They were exploring each other, learning and claiming and taking.

When she couldn't stand it anymore, when the wave overtook her and carried him with it, she pressed her lips to his to stop *I love you* from tumbling free.

He didn't have to hear it. She'd already told him with her body, with her gasps and her sharp nails and slick heat welcoming him again and again.

She might need to think, but her body did not. It had chosen him. Was still choosing him. Would never stop choosing him over anything else.

When he collapsed in her arms, as breathless and sated as she, he rolled over to his back, keeping her locked in his embrace, until the ear he had kissed so tenderly rested atop the comforting beat of his heart.

"Thaddeus?" she whispered.

He mumbled something incomprehensible into the top of her head.

She smiled against the warmth of his chest and cradled the side of his face in her hand.

He pressed a kiss to her palm and didn't move.

Tomorrow, she would tell him. After he'd gone home, after she'd had the night to think it over, when he came for his answer and she still said yes, he would know it was really true, and not a flash of emotion.

She'd thought her only future was a life of riches and loneliness, of endless adventure but no one to share it with. She'd begun to fear she'd never find love, that she didn't *deserve* love, that it was a pretty story that never came true.

And then came Thaddeus. Time after time, she'd pushed him away, forcing him out before he could leave her on his own, knowing that when he did, it would destroy her.

But he didn't leave. Was right here in her arms. Willing to share them with her for the rest of their lives.

How could she say no to an adventure like that?

CHAPTER 13

*T*had spent the following morning selecting and discarding various waist-coats and neckcloths, followed by an equally frenetic trip to the market for fresh flowers that would convey the perfect message.

Not a limp handful of wilting daffodils. Something that said *I love you* and I *want you* and *Marry me…* but not florid or pushy or impatient.

Priscilla had asked for time to think. She had said "at least tomorrow." Arriving at her doorstep at half past eleven in the morning with a mixed bouquet of roses and spring flowers in his hand did not mean an answer would be waiting for him.

Thad was prepared to give her time. And room to think, if that was what she wanted. But he didn't want her to fear for a single second that his affection had waned after sharing her bed. Last night would be the first of many.

He pulled onto Grosvenor Square with a silly

smile taking over his face. All at once, his giddiness turned into confusion.

A strange carriage was parked in the spot right across from her door, the spot Thad had come to think of as *his*.

"Carriage" was not the right term.

This was a gorgeous coal-black cabriolet, pulled by the most stunning pure white Arabian. Thad had never seen such a lovely animal, or a carriage so clean and sharp it looked as though it had sprung from a picture book rather than out of London's dirty streets.

Indeed, it was the sort of horse and carriage Thad always imagined himself riding in on, when he came to whisk his lady fair away to their happy ending.

He pulled his gig to a stop behind the cabriolet.

No footmen rushed out to greet him.

Thad leapt from his carriage, muddying his painstakingly shined boots in the process, and tied his horse to the closest post.

Still no footmen.

He collected the flowers from the gig and trudged up the walk to the front door.

It remained closed.

He shifted his flowers into his other hand and gave the knocker a sharp rap. And another. And one more for good measure.

The butler did not swing open the door with his usual alacrity.

The butler did not answer the door at all.

Thad glanced over his shoulder, certain everyone on the square was watching him, flowers in hand, as his knocks went unanswered.

Didn't both owners of the Wicked Duke live on this square? Thad's chest tightened. He was never going to hear the end of this humiliation.

He gave the knocker another go, perhaps a touch more frantic than before.

This time, after the most interminable of pauses, the butler opened the door.

"Yes?" he said abstractedly, without even looking at Thad.

It did not signify. Thad was not here to see the butler. He straightened his spine.

"Miss Weatherby, if you please," he said crisply.

"Oh," the butler said. "I am sure she is not receiving."

Not receiving because she did not wish to see Thad? Or not receiving for some other reason? The sort of reason that rode up on a white horse with a fairy book cabriolet?

"Could you perhaps *enquire* whether she is receiving?" Thad asked politely.

"Oh," the butler said again. "I really think I couldn't. Her father has come, and it's put the house in a bit of a tizzy. Could you call another day?"

No, Thad realized. He really couldn't.

"Her *father* came for her?" he repeated blankly. Her father, the grand adventurer. The flowers in Thad's hands felt impossibly heavy.

Of all the scenarios he had played out in his mind between yesterday and this morning, Priscilla's father returning to whisk her away to adventure was not one of them.

It hadn't even crossed Thad's mind. How could it?

There was the trust to consider, the question of whether either of them could wait until her twenty-fifth birthday for the inheritance—and whether it was ethical to do so, even if every penny went to Priscilla—and of course the sort of cold feet anyone might get when her life's dream was to go on adventures with her father, and all she got instead was Thad and a rented townhouse and a cat named Wednesday.

He had thought Priscilla was deciding between him and some nebulous future adventure that she may or may not take, because even if she remained a spinster and inherited a million coffers of gold coin, a secret part of Thad had thought—had wished—had *hoped* she wouldn't do it. Had hoped she *couldn't* do it.

If not because of her love for him, then at least because a woman traveling alone in far-flung lands was not the safest situation and—

And none of it mattered because she *wasn't* alone. She *didn't* need to wait. She could have the adventures right now.

She didn't need Thad.

"Sir?" the butler asked, his brow furrowed in obvious concern.

Thad shook his head. He did not trust himself to speak. Besides, what was there to say?

Priscilla was Princess Charming. Of that, Thad was certain. The problem appeared to be that *he* wasn't her prince.

Her story appeared to involve the man she'd dreamed would fetch her since childhood after all. The criminally absent father who, despite all the odds, had turned up at the last moment just in time to cock up Thad's wedding proposal.

All he could do was let his princess sail off to find the happy ever after she deserved.

"Not receiving," he said aloud, lowering his flowers. "I understand."

The door began to close before he'd even turned away.

Just before it clicked shut inches from Thad's face, the door flung back open wide.

There she was. Priscilla. Looking resplendent in high color and chestnut curls and eyes that sparkled just like the sea that would carry her away.

She bit her lip. "Thaddeus."

Thaddeus.

Just one word, and yet it seemed to convey that everything was indeed falling apart, just as it seemed. Even the air around them was thick and heavy and suffocating.

"*Ma chérie,*" he said, and lifted the flowers. "I came—"

"I know what you came to ask." Her eyes were haunted, pleading, but she did not take the flowers. "I… can't right now. My father's here. I'm sorry."

"I'm sorry, too," he said as she shut the door.

It was true. He had never been sorrier in all his life. It felt like his heart was dying, rotting his chest from the inside out.

I can't right now wasn't *yes* or *no*, which was somehow even worse than an answer. Or perhaps it was the answer. Because the future Priscilla had been waiting on had just arrived.

As Thad trudged back to his gig, he tossed the bouquet of carefully chosen flowers onto the bench of the cabriolet. That's where they belonged. Everyone knew beautiful white horses were for the hero of the story.

He wasn't even part of the plot.

CHAPTER 14

*P*riscilla closed the front door and hurried to reopen the door to the parlor.

Guilt squeezed her heart. She hated seeing the happy hopefulness on Thaddeus's face crumble so completely. She could welcome him inside and tell him what he wanted to hear. That she knew what to tell him, what to say, what to do.

But everyone was saying far too many words this morning. Another visitor had arrived not a quarter hour before him, while Priscilla was upstairs being dressed. Her maid had glimpsed the carriage while she was tying Priscilla's stays.

They didn't recognize the cabriolet, couldn't see the passengers disembark from inside her dressing room, but something awful was happening. Raised voices trickled up through the floor, followed by the slam of a door.

She had flown downstairs with no shoes and half-finished curls, just in time to glimpse Thaddeus. He was not the cause of the commotion. The other guest was still inside. Muffled shouting from inside the front parlor was audible despite the closed door.

Priscilla could not abandon her grandmother to face another minute of such mistreatment alone.

On shaking limbs, she yanked open the door to the parlor and dashed inside.

Her stockinged feet slid to a halt on the carpet, nearly catapulting her arse-over-teakettle upon sight of the scene inside. Someone *new* was in the parlor again. No... someone old.

"Papa?" she stuttered in wondrous disbelief.

But of course it was Papa. Ten years might pass, twenty, thirty, but she would recognize him anywhere. The same shock of graying hair, the same ruddy cheeks and animated features, the same too-bright eyes that always seemed lit from within. Right now, those eyes were focused on Grandmother.

She did not appear thrilled at her son's renewed presence in their home. She looked disgusted with him. Furious. She was on her feet before him, her pale hands curving into claws at her thin sides. Even out of the oversized chair she spent her days in, Grandmother was dwarfed by his presence. But she wasn't backing down.

"How dare you," she snarled, regal despite obvious anger. "Why the devil are you here?"

The only times Priscilla had ever heard her

grandmother invoke the devil was when she was talking about her son.

Priscilla rushed over to position herself between them like a shield.

"He's here to visit. To ensure everything is going to plan," she said soothingly, only for a wonderful, terrible, miraculous idea to crowd out the rest. She spun to face her father, excitement racing through her veins like wildfire. "Or he's come to fetch me early."

His lively blue eyes wavered for only a moment before a smile overtook his face. "Daughter?"

Of course she was his daughter. But years had passed since he had seen her last. Her mourning dress was gone, as were her schoolgirl ringlets, and her innocence.

She was older now. Stronger, wiser. More experienced. More resilient. But still Priscilla.

"It's me," she said, her pleading voice breaking on the words. *Recognize me. Love me.*

Every time she'd imagined their reunion, Papa was always thrilled to see her. He would recognize her immediately and hold out his arms. She would rush into them as she always had done, and he would swing her around in joy before whispering, *Send for your trunk. You're coming with me.*

Nothing was going to plan.

"You're lovely," Papa said, although this could not possibly be true. Her hair was half-curled and her slippers were somewhere upstairs but maybe, to a father, one's daughter was always beautiful no matter what.

"She's three-and-twenty," Grandmother snapped. "A grown woman."

"A grown woman," he repeated, and seemed to rethink Priscilla's words. His eyes crinkled affably. "Of course you're welcome to come with me. Are you ready for adventure?"

Not *precisely* the way she'd imagined this conversation unfolding, but the important bits were there all the same. He was here. He'd come back. He wanted to take her with him.

Was she ready for adventure? She'd dreamt of nothing else her entire life.

"Aren't you going to ask how she's been all these years?" Grandmother snapped.

"Stop it," Priscilla hissed.

"We'll have plenty of time to chat on the journey," Papa said, still staring at Priscilla as if he couldn't quite credit the evidence standing before his eyes.

Grandmother glared down her nose at him. "What about her husband and three children?"

Papa's jaw dropped in shock. "She's married?"

"Of course I'm not married," Priscilla spluttered. What sense would that make? Grandmother was trying to cause trouble for some reason. "Haven't you been receiving my letters?"

The confusion cleared from her father's face. "Oh, we're not in Africa anymore. From there, we went to the Seychelles and then settled in India. Next, I've my eye on Brazil. Fascinating country."

She had no doubt, although her head was spinning from everywhere he'd been, and she hadn't even known. Her letters hadn't come back. They were probably lying in a pile in some dusty post-house. Or in a fire, keeping the postmaster warm.

"Where's Grandfather?" she asked.

Grandmother tensed, as if the answer would flay the flesh from her bones.

Priscilla gaped at her, startled. All that shouting… She'd assumed a row about Grandfather was at the heart of it. "You didn't *ask?*"

"He's in India," Papa said with a chuckle. "I doubt I'll ever get him out of there. The beautiful weather, the gorgeous food, so many delightful… charms. It's heaven on earth."

Grandmother no longer seemed solid. As though she'd been burnt into a hollow husk of herself, a grandmother-shaped curl of ash that would disintegrate in the next puff of wind and scatter into nothing.

That was why she hadn't asked, Priscilla realized. He wasn't here. He hadn't come. There was nothing else Grandmother needed to know.

"I can't stay long," Papa said.

Priscilla turned to him in shock. "Surely, a few weeks—"

"I must present myself at port this afternoon, or the boat will leave without me," he said, as if it was all a simple matter of practicality.

"But you just got here," she protested.

Grandmother's sad eyes met hers, and Priscilla

tried not to crumble. Papa had only just arrived *here*, in their drawing room, at their town house, but his boat had docked at port who knew how many days or weeks before. They were an afterthought, at best.

But he *had* come.

"Well, daughter." Oblivious, Papa turned his jovial gaze to Priscilla. "Care to accompany an old man off to adventure? Can you have a trunk packed by two o'clock?"

She'd kept a trunk packed since she was nine. It could be downstairs within minutes.

Her throat was dry, her palms sweaty. The moment was finally here. Fate, knocking at her door, as Thaddeus might say.

She closed her eyes.

In all her imaginings of sailing off to adventure with her father, never once had the vision entailed leaving the man she loved behind.

Worse. Priscilla opened her eyes. Whether she went or stayed, she would be saying goodbye to someone she loved.

She'd told Thaddeus from the beginning that she didn't want a husband and never would. That what they had was temporary. She'd fallen in love with him, *made* love with him, but hadn't made any promises or indicated it would be for more than one night.

Thaddeus wanted far more than one night. He wanted love. He wanted forever. He wanted a wife and a family and a home here in London. He wanted Priscilla.

Her chest pounded in misery and panic.

Papa wouldn't be back for another decade or two, if then. Priscilla could set out as soon as she had her inheritance, but she wouldn't have the least idea where to find him. Perhaps he'd be in India or Brazil. Perhaps he wouldn't.

If she was ever going to join her father and grandfather on their journeys, this was her one and only chance.

She turned to her grandmother.

Grandmother's eyes were open and focused, glassy and fierce. Her chin held high, her spine impossibly straight, her mouth a thin line. She'd known how this conversation would go even before Priscilla walked in the door.

Her stomach churned. Priscilla didn't want to be like her grandmother, refused to be anything at all like Mama, but did she truly wish to be cut from the same cloth as her father and grandfather?

They chose adventure over love. Themselves over family. Self-indulgence over true connection.

They were happy, Priscilla had no doubt. But following them wouldn't be forging her own way. Sailing off with her father and grandfather wouldn't be realizing her dreams, but theirs. It was time she picked her own.

Love was scarier than adventure. Marriage was positively terrifying. Risking her heart, risking her happiness, risking her future, was what she had meticulously avoided doing all these lonely years.

She couldn't leave Thaddeus behind, like her father and grandfather had done to her. Not just because she knew how awful that felt, but because *Thaddeus* was un-leave-behind-able. Marriage wasn't a prison sentence, but a partnership.

Priscilla's worst fear was being abandoned. Forgotten. Her goal had never been to live on ships and horses the rest of her life, but rather not to be left behind.

That was exactly what Thaddeus had been offering her. He wanted to take her with him for the rest of their lives, into a future they determined together. *He* was what made thoughts of the future joyful.

A temporary liaison wasn't good enough. One night of love could never suffice. She wanted forever.

She wanted Thaddeus.

"No," she said aloud, the word strong and forceful and sure.

There was something new in the parlor again. This time, it was Priscilla. Taking over the reins of her life.

"No?" Her father reared back as if he'd never before been on the receiving end of the word. Perhaps he hadn't.

It was time.

"No," Priscilla repeated. "I'm not going with you."

Not this time, not ever. Even if it meant

giving up her inheritance. Even if it meant disappointing her father. Losing his respect. His love.

Grandmother turned to her in bewilderment. "No?"

"No," Priscilla said again. The word was terrifying and freeing. *No* was final. Decision made.

"But," Grandmother stammered. "Adventure..."

Priscilla touched her grandmother's pale hand and gave a crooked smile. "We'll always have Koffi."

"Coffee?" Papa laughed as if the very idea was vulgar and naïve. "If you could taste the chai in India, you'd never—"

"Not 'coffee,'" Priscilla said. "*Koffi.* The parrot you brought me from Africa."

After Mama died.

"Did I?" His confusion gave way to amusement. "What a lark! I thought we'd lost that thing."

Every bone in her body trembled with hurt and disappointment. That moment had been the biggest turning point in Priscilla's life, and he didn't even remember. His visit that year had been the one bright light in the spiraling darkness... and it hadn't meant anything to him at all.

"Have a good trip," she said, and meant it. She was glad he was leaving today. "I'll be married by the time you reach India."

"You'll be what?" he said, perplexed. "I thought you said—"

"She has a suitor," Grandmother said with pride. "A fine man who loves her."

Priscilla looked at her in surprise. "How do you know he loves me?"

"Who wouldn't?" Grandmother's voice was gruff, but her gaze was tender. "And he keeps coming back."

Papa frowned. "Do you need me to sign something?"

"I'm three-and-twenty," she reminded him. She had her majority. What she wouldn't have was the inheritance. "Don't worry about the trust."

"The...trust?" he echoed in bafflement.

Grandmother closed her eyes.

"The trust," Priscilla repeated, lightheaded with something akin to panic. "The one you set up for me in case I was still unwed on my twenty-fifth birthday. Ten thousand pounds in my name."

"I remember now." Papa chuckled. "I'm glad you've brought some chap up to scratch. I *meant* to set aside that inheritance—"

"Just like you meant to leave her a dowry?" Grandmother snapped.

"I didn't do that, either?" he asked in surprise. He sent them both an oh-well, what-can-you-do grin. "Of course any daughter of mine would be enchanting with or without a piece of paper."

"It's not a piece of paper," Priscilla gritted out through clenched teeth. "A dowry is how a woman can influence her future. That inheritance was supposed to be my *freedom*. That money—"

But it wasn't the money. It had never been the money.

The trust had always been a symbol. Proof that her father loved her. Proof that he remembered her, thought about her. Proof that he was waiting for her.

And it had always been a lie.

"You knew," she accused her grandmother, voice bleak. "You knew and you didn't tell me."

"I didn't want to break your heart." Her grandmother's gaze was tortured. "You had just lost your mother. Who knew if your father would ever return? If you needed to believe in a fairy-tale to get through each day, I wasn't going to rip that from you, too."

Priscilla's heart skipped. "But you told me—"

"I told you, *Get married.*" Grandmother's eyes flashed. "It was your only chance for a better life. A chance for happiness. There was no trust, no dowry. Just an old townhouse with an old woman inside." She suddenly seemed small and frail. "One bitter old lady is enough. I didn't want that for *you.*"

"Don't be bitter." Priscilla wrapped her in a fierce hug. "I told you. I'll never abandon you. I'm yours forever. You're my grandmother, and I love you."

"You made the right decision by choosing love," Grandmother whispered into her hair.

"*That's* the man who deserves you. You didn't give up anything at all."

Priscilla pulled away in horror. She'd closed the door on the man who loved her. He'd come for an answer, and that had been her response. She would not blame him if he no longer trusted her love, no longer was interested in risking his future on a woman who would shut the door against him when all he ever wanted from her was her love.

"Go," Grandmother said as if reading her thoughts. "Get him."

Priscilla nodded and ran from the parlor without even sparing a glance at her father. He was her past.

Thaddeus was her future.

CHAPTER 15

*T*had scanned his bedchamber bookshelves, determined to pretend everything was fine. He armed himself with his favorite biographies and nestled in his usual chair located in the same corner of his iron balcony. Life would go on as normal.

Except it didn't feel normal. It felt like the ague and influenza and the morning after a long night of far too much whisky.

Thunder crashed overhead and the first wave of mottled clouds spit cold drops of rain onto Thad's shoulders. Fitting.

He could let himself be sad that Priscilla preferred a life of surprises and excitement and adventure, but he could not be surprised.

She had *told* him she didn't want a husband. She had *told* him their bluebirds-singing, rainbows-soaring, fireworks-exploding liaison could only be temporary.

She had told him he might have his answer in the morning.

He opened a book at random, uncaring which end was up. Nothing else was going the right way, so why should this biography on Jean-Jacques Rousseau be any different? Its lengthy paragraphs slowly came into focus. Not Rousseau. *Africa.* In Thad's distracted state, he'd chosen books that reminded him of Priscilla.

"*Damn* it." He flung them inside the room, heedless of where or how they might land.

Normally, when he wanted to escape from the world into something that brought him joy and peace, Thad picked up a pencil and his journal and got lost in his manuscript.

He didn't *have* his manuscript. He'd given it to Priscilla along with his heart.

Not that he felt like working on it. Thad didn't feel like anything at all. He propped his elbows on his knees and dropped his face into his palms.

He would simply have to keep his distance, he decided dully. An effortless proposition, given Priscilla's father was here to whisk her to exotic locales on the other side of the globe.

Thad would simply continue on as usual. The same tavern. The same chair. The same routine, the same routs, the same smile plastered on his face as he invited the same people to the same dances.

No matter how splintered his heart might feel inside.

He might have passed the entire day like that —head in hands, elbows digging into knees, spine slumped, heart heavy—were it not for a commotion on the street below.

Worried a carriage accident might be unfolding right outside his door, he leapt to his feet at once.

Carriage, yes.

Accident, no.

It was the polished ebony cabriolet, with its shining wheels and spotless leather harness and its majestic white Arabian stallion, fit for a hero. But Priscilla's father was not at the reins.

The woman he loved slid awkwardly from the cab in a flutter of flower petals and expensive silk, to land—stocking-footed?—on the street below.

"Thaddeus Middleton," she called up, lilting voice strong and pure. "You have something that belongs to me."

His fingers gripped the iron railing as he stared down at her.

Half her hair was in perfect ringlets. The other half looked as though it had lost a battle with her parrot.

She had never been more beautiful.

Even his neighbors were hanging out windows to watch.

"What do you want?" he shouted. Or meant to shout. He wasn't certain his voice had carried over the sound of the falling rain and the pounding of his heart.

"*You.*" Her eyes sparkled as she gazed up at him. "There is no one else I want. You possess my heart."

"I don't have much else," he called back. "This townhouse is rented, and my gig—"

"I'm not in love with a house or a carriage," she called back. "I'm in love with *you*. Nothing else matters."

He tried to contain a dangerous wave of wonderful, breathless hope.

"You say that today," he pointed out with resignation. "But what about tomorrow, or next year, or the decade after that, when your love turns into resentment for stealing you away from all the things you want more?"

"There is *nothing* I want more," she said fiercely, her eyes at once determined and beseeching. "You are my first and only choice. Anything else would be settling for less."

He wished he could believe that. "What about your father?"

"Papa's here," she said with a lift of her shoulder. "He'll be gone by nightfall. He invited me to join him, but why would I? I'd miss the best part." Her gaze never strayed from his. "The real adventure is a life here with you."

"Here?" he said doubtfully, gesturing behind him.

"No matter what the guidebooks say," she told him, "there is no mystical utopia hiding in the jungle. Any place can be paradise if we make it so. For me, that place is wherever you happen to be."

"I can't afford to spend every day of the year traveling," he reminded her. Like she'd told him from the first: *you don't have what I need.* "And I wouldn't wish to be unmoored forever."

"That was my misconception," she admitted. "I thought I had to choose one or the other. I didn't realize I could have a home *and* adventure. I didn't know I could have love… and take it with me."

More windows flung open as people openly gawked at the street.

His hands gripped the iron railing as hope fluttered within him. "You'd like a home *and* adventure?"

She turned to the carriage, pulled a book from the squab, and held it high over her head with both hands. "See this?"

He didn't need to browse the words inside to know it was the half-finished biography he'd started to write about her. Part One, before the intrepid adventuress was famous.

"You were right," she called up. "The story is only half over. But 'part two' isn't about me. It's about *us.* There is no adventure worth having if it doesn't involve both of us together."

It was as if she was reading the words right from his heart. There was nothing he wanted more than to spend every moment of forever with her.

Still holding the journal aloft, she raised her

voice for all to hear. "Thaddeus Middleton, *mon chéri, gardien de mon cœur*. Will you join me in a love story we write ourselves?"

Joy flooded him. She meant every word. She loved him. *He* was the adventure she chose. *We. Us.* The white stallion had been a sign after all:

They were the heroes of their own story.

CHAPTER 16

*P*riscilla stood in the middle of the street, arms in the air, holding the book aloft.

After a lifetime of trying to stay out of sight and away from wagging tongues, she was now singlehandedly causing the scandal of the season.

She had stolen a carriage to come shout from the street... with no shoes, half her hair curled, and her heart at her feet. There was only one man she could not let get away. She didn't want to waste another moment without Thad by her side.

If he still wanted her.

He'd been staring down at her with an aching mix of love and hurt and hope and doubt.

Belatedly, she realized she'd forgotten the most important words of all.

She tucked the journal back under the squab and hiked up her hems in preparation for sinking to one knee.

"Thaddeus Middleton," she began.

Before she could so much as bend, he dropped from the balcony and landed on his feet before her with a slow, devastating smile.

"Wait," he said and pulled her into his embrace. "It's my question."

She wrapped her arms about his neck and held on tight. "My answer is yes."

He grinned at her. "I haven't asked you yet."

"You asked yesterday," she reminded him. "And the answer is yes. Yes today, yes tomorrow, yes forever. I'm yours for as long as you want me."

"I'll want you forever," he said and touched his forehead to hers.

Thunder crackled overhead and the sky fell down to greet them.

Priscilla pushed a matted tendril out of her eyes and blinked up at the rain. "Maybe we'll see a rainbow."

"Who needs to wait for that?" Thaddeus answered and slanted his mouth over hers.

This kiss was different than all the rest. It wasn't shy and exploring, or bold and adventurous, but sweet and sensual. A mutual claiming, a romance of tongues and a meeting of hearts.

There was nothing to prove. Just joy to share. She loved him. He loved her. They belonged together. This was the first day of forever.

He swung her up into the carriage.

She blinked down at him in surprise. "What are you doing?"

"*We*," he said as he hoisted himself up beside her, "are going to do things right."

He made a gesture toward the front door of his townhouse, where his maids had gathered to watch the proceedings.

A footman came loping over. "Yes, sir?"

"Follow us in the gig, please," Thaddeus instructed him, then turned to give Priscilla another kiss. "This is my chance to officially ask for your hand while your father is still here." He stroked the satin squab with obvious reluctance. "And also return a stolen carriage."

She grinned at him. "I'm not sorry."

"Neither am I," he admitted, grinning right back.

They were halfway to Grosvenor Square when she remembered she hadn't told him the entire story.

"There's no money," she forced herself to admit, anger still mixing with hurt. "No inheritance. There never was."

"I never cared," he said softly, his brown eyes full of nothing but love. "All I ever wanted is you."

She slipped her hand into his.

He pressed a kiss to her hair. "And maybe shoes. Yes, the more I think about it, I've always yearned for a wife with shoes."

"That's a very specific wish." She handed him his journal. "Quite superficial of you. Not unconditional love at all. Wednesday doesn't wear shoes. Koffi doesn't wear shoes."

"If you sprout fur or feathers, you can stop

181

wearing shoes, too," he promised her. "Or we can never leave the bedchamber. I have never heard of a finer reason to neglect practical footwear."

"Excellent point," she agreed, and snuggled into his warm side. "I accept your offer."

But the bedchamber would have to wait. When they pulled onto Grosvenor Square, Priscilla's father was standing on the front step with an umbrella in one hand and a pocket watch in the other.

She tensed, expecting the sight of his obvious hurry to leave to break her heart anew, as it always had done.

This time, it did not.

He was not a god, an angel of adventure, a wise man on a mountaintop that must be scaled in order to deserve peace.

He was just a man. A flawed one, a selfish one. This time when he left, she would not miss him.

Thaddeus leapt to the ground, then held up his arms for her.

She went into them eagerly.

"I also dreamed of joining my wife in a hot bath," he whispered into her ear as she slid down beside him.

Her cheeks flushed with heat. Marriage would be full of adventures, indeed.

"I got your carriage muddy," she told her father when he didn't speak.

"Priscilla…" he said at last.

He was looking at her with a mix of amusement and admiration. And perhaps a little regret.

"Here." Papa returned his timepiece to his pocket and shoved a few pound notes in her direction. "Take this. It's not ten thousand, but it's what I have handy. I'll set you up with a proper account the next time I'm in London."

Sure he would. Priscilla would not hold her breath.

Thaddeus cleared his throat. "Sir, I—"

But Papa was already swinging himself into the cabriolet, reaching for his reins, spurring his horse.

"Do a better job than I did," he said as the wheels took him away. "Never let her forget that you love her."

Thaddeus turned to Priscilla in disappointment. "I wasn't able to finish the question."

"He'll be back in twelve years," she assured him wryly. "Or perhaps not."

Thaddeus took her hands in his and lifted them to his lips. "How are *you* taking this?"

"Actually..." She glanced at the wrinkled bills in her hands, then gave him a lopsided smile. "Not bad, I think. We have money! Ten whole pounds. How miffed would you be if I spent it on shoes?"

"Exceedingly unmiffed," he assured her. "You may be interested to learn that I have money, too."

She narrowed her eyes. "You found a shilling on the pavements?"

"Is that where shillings come from?" he fired back with an expression of wide-eyed innocence.

"I have two thousand pounds a year. Not riches, you might think, if it must cover two people, and perhaps you would be right. But what you may *not* know is that I've only been spending half, and saving the other. Since I inherited when I was twelve and have just turned eight-and-twenty, that should be… oh, dear, I find mathematics so very tedious…"

"You have *sixteen thousand pounds?*" she spluttered in disbelief.

"That's the number!" he agreed cheerfully. "Do you mind if I commission a pair of shoes, too?"

"But—Thaddeus—" she stuttered. "Do you know what this means?"

"It means," he said as he swung her into his arms, "We can have a honeymoon anywhere in the world you please. We can take your bird, my cat, your grandmother, the whole family. We can even go…" He wiggled his eyebrows and gave a suggestive leer. "…*footwear optional.*"

"We're going footwear optional right this minute," she said as she dragged him back to the street toward their waiting carriage. "As your future wife, I demand a tour of your bedchamber."

"That's not all I'll give you," he promised wickedly, and set off to prove just that.

EPILOGUE

30 July, 1818
Weatherby Townhouse
Grosvenor Square, London, England

*P*riscilla threw back her head and laughed at the sight of so many people crowded into her grandmother's front parlor.

"A surprise party?" she said in glee. "For me?"

"Happy birthday, you impossible creature," her husband growled affectionately.

Thaddeus had no doubt played an important part in the soirée, but he had not done so alone.

Grandmother sat in her oversized chair with an equally oversized smile of satisfaction curving her lips.

The parlor was no longer dark, but filled with light and life and love... and dozens of new artifacts. They hadn't yet reached Africa, but they'd spent their honeymoon on the Continent *en famille*, picking up gewgaws and miniature paintings everywhere they went.

Koffi was not in his cage, but perched atop a curtain rod. An exemplary vantage point from which to monitor not only the festivities below, but also the activities of a certain black-and-white cat darting from boot to slipper in search of fallen crumbs.

Rather than develop a taste for sweets herself, Wednesday had discovered the parrot could not resist the allure of a strategically placed morsel— placing his tail-feathers in perfect range for a playful bat of Wednesday's paw.

Priscilla could scarcely credit that she had once hoped to spend her twenty-fifth birthday on a six-month voyage in search of two men who had become strangers.

Instead, she was in her grandmother's home, surrounded by all her friends and the people she loved most.

She and Thaddeus had purchased a beautiful cottage in the country, with more than enough room for her grandmother and two pets and plenty of children. Not a single one would be left behind on any holiday, no matter where the family might roam.

Thaddeus swung her behind a folding screen to steal a quick kiss. "Did you get everything you wanted for your birthday?"

"You gave me my present sixteen months ago," she said with a grin.

"I did?" His brow furrowed. "What was it?"

She wrapped her arms about him and whispered, "You gave me happy ever after."

The kiss he gave her in reply proved that this was only the beginning.

THE END

~

THANK YOU FOR READING

Love talking books with fellow readers?

Join the *Historical Romance Book Club* for prizes, books, and live chats with your favorite romance authors:

Facebook.com/groups/HistRomBookClub

Check out the *12 Dukes of Christmas* facebook group for giveaways and exclusive content:

Facebook.com/groups/DukesOfChristmas

Join the *Rogues to Riches* facebook group for insider info and first looks at future books in the series:

Facebook.com/groups/RoguesToRiches

Check out the *Dukes of War* facebook group for giveaways and exclusive content:

Facebook.com/groups/DukesOfWar

And check out the official website for sneak peeks and more:

www.EricaRidley.com/books

Don't forget your free book!

Sign up at http://ridley.vip for members-only exclusives, including advance notice of pre-orders, as well as contests, giveaways, freebies, and 99¢ deals!

In order, the *Wicked Dukes Club*:

One Night for Seduction by Erica Ridley
One Night of Surrender by Darcy Burke
One Night of Passion by Erica Ridley
One Night of Scandal by Darcy Burke
One Night to Remember by Erica Ridley
One Night of Temptation by Darcy Burke

In order, the *12 Dukes of Christmas*:
Once Upon a Duke
Kiss of a Duke
Wish Upon a Duke
Never Say Duke
Dukes, Actually
The Duke's Bride
The Duke's Embrace
The Duke's Desire
Dawn With a Duke
One Night With a Duke
Ten Days With a Duke
Forever Your Duke

～

In order, the *Rogues to Riches* books are:
Lord of Chance
Lord of Pleasure
Lord of Night
Lord of Temptation
Lord of Secrets
Lord of Vice

～

In order, the *Dukes of War* books are:
The Viscount's Tempting Minx (FREE!)
The Earl's Defiant Wallflower
The Captain's Bluestocking Mistress
The Major's Faux Fiancée

The Brigadier's Runaway Bride
The Pirate's Tempting Stowaway
The Duke's Accidental Wife

ACKNOWLEDGMENTS

As always, I could not have written this book without the invaluable support of my critique partner, beta readers, and editors. Huge thanks go out to Darcy Burke, Tessa Shapcott, Erica Monroe, and Tracy Emro. You are the best!

Lastly, I want to thank the *Historical Romance Book Club* facebook group and my fabulous street team. Your enthusiasm makes the romance happen.

Thank you so much!

ABOUT THE AUTHOR

Erica Ridley is a *New York Times* and *USA Today* best-selling author of historical romance novels.

In the new *Rogues to Riches* historical romance series, Cinderella stories aren't just for princesses… Sigh-worthy Regency rogues sweep strong-willed young ladies into whirlwind rags-to-riches romance with rollicking adventure.

The popular *Dukes of War* series features roguish peers and dashing war heroes who return from battle only to be thrust into the splendor and madness of Regency England.

When not reading or writing romances, Erica can be found riding camels in Africa, zip-lining through rainforests in Central America, or getting hopelessly lost in the middle of Budapest.

~

Let's be friends! Find Erica on:
www.EricaRidley.com

Made in the USA
Middletown, DE
20 May 2019